D0710602

FREAK WEATHER

Kuryla, Mary,author.
Freak weather :stories

2017
33305239963741
mi   12/27/17

FREAK WEATHER

STORIES

MARY KURYLA

University of Massachusetts Press
Amherst and Boston

This book is the winner of the 2016 Grace Paley Prize in Short Fiction. The Association of Writers & Writing Programs, which sponsors the award, is a national nonprofit organization dedicated to serving American letters, writers, and programs of writing. Its headquarters are at George Mason University, Fairfax, Virginia, and its website is www.awpwriter.org.

Copyright © 2017 by Mary Kuryla
All rights reserved
Printed in the United States of America

ISBN 978-1-62534-307-9 (pbk)

Set in Adobe Garamond Pro and Unboring
Printed and bound by Sheridan Books, Inc.

Jacket photo by Kathleen Prati.

Library of Congress Cataloging-in-Publication Data

Names: Kuryla, Mary, author.
Title: Freak weather : stories / Mary Kuryla.
Description: Amherst : University Of Massachusetts Press, 2017. | Series:
Grace Paley Prize in Short Fiction | Published in cooperation with
Association of Writers and Writing Programs — Publisher's note.
Identifiers: LCCN 2017020930 | ISBN 9781625343079 (jacketed cloth)
Classification: LCC PS3611.U7345 A6 2017 | DDC 813/.6—dc23

LC record available at https://lccn.loc.gov/2017020930
British Library Cataloguing-in-Publication Data

The Grace Paley Prize in Short Fiction is made possible
by the generous support of Amazon.com.

Freak Weather 1

So Now Sorrow 13

The Way of Affliction 23

Deaf Dog 43

Animal Control 51

In Our House 69

Mis-sayings 79

To Skin a Rabbit 93

My Husband's Son 105

Introduction to Feathers 121

The Worst of You 135

What's to Light 147

Not in Nottingham 157

Acknowledgments 173

FREAK WEATHER

ONLY THE BOSS IS AT THE STATION WHEN I roll up. All I am after is my fellow's money, what he earned fair and square. The boss knows it. He's writing out the check already.

"Make it out to Jim?" Bob says.

"Make it out to me," I say.

He's tearing out the check when he asks if my shorts are called hot pants.

"I put them on because it felt like spring," I say, "a spring calf."

"Yeah?" he says. "It's been cold as hell." He looks out the window, like maybe he can see some of what's circulating in the air. When he turns back, his smile is all sly boots. "The weather has turned on you," Bob says.

I take the paycheck and even though our business is done, I don't go. That puts more on his mind. Not like I didn't see what was on his mind every time I stopped by the gas station asking for Jimmy. Only this is the opportunity. Nobody's around. Could close up shop. What we couldn't do.

Bob starts snapping off lights. He's no thick-in-the-head like my fellow. Outside it's plain cold. Bob drops the station key in a pocket and says, "I've got some venison steaks. That could warm you up."

"The dog's in the car," I say. "So's the pizza. It's dinner." I don't say how Jimmy's home waiting on me to deliver. Bob can figure that out.

He says, "Playing hard to get?"

What it is, I just remembered about my dog when I saw the car windows gone foggy. We go unroll a window and look at Mink in the back seat, watching that bit of tail shudder. Bob drops his head on my shoulder, a head with an odor of uncut lawn, and he says, "That's an old dog. What kind of dog is that?" I say what kind of dog—not that it matters. Old dogs look very much alike.

Bob says he's got most all of a bottle at home and he knows how to come by something smokeable but it's not cheap. "You make a budget," he says. I tell the snake to cash Jimmy's paycheck, and we go back inside the station that is not yet cold.

Lights stay off even though he's making change at the register. Sheets of sun-filter bring twilight in more purply than it is outside. I keep watch on Bob's forearms, wrists, and the thumb that counts out twenties, the tens, the ones. Bob probably crowing inside that it's the last pay Jimmy will see from him.

I don't get the money all the way in my purse before starting on kissing him. He is that good a kisser. A pang in my stomach when he yanks me in. There's the cot in the room back the garage, the one I napped on waiting on Jimmy, but Bob says, "Let's eat deer."

"You eat pizza if you don't like it," Bob says, stepping inside his home. He says, "Venison, that's acquired taste."

Eaten plenty of it already. My first pop from a 30-06 brought a stag to its knees, but I'm not saying. Why not let Bob feel he's got a real treat.

"Warm yourself," he says, preparing to leave me in this home that's only a home as far as something pitched on wheels is. "Scoot up to the heater air."

I can't go with Bob. He says his friend gets funny around new faces, but it's not his friend. It's Bob who's still got the thinking that dope's a secret to keep until you're one with the dirty earth. He's using my car, traveling incognito, and so I say, "Make a window crack for the dog."

"Snow might get in," he says.

I say, "If that's what the weather has a mind to do."

Bob is gone too long and I watch snow come down in fists, thinking of my daffodils, my yellow blooms blooming all day yesterday. I knew they were too good to be good. I'd text Bob to hurry it up, but he doesn't sport a phone. Plays it incognito. Such a fuss. The smokeable he's purchasing from his funny friend better not be of crack variety. If Bob hadn't taken my car, I'd mosey on out of here, back to where he'd be, sitting the couch and waiting on me to do his dirty work and calling it babysitting. That chicken shit. It's fowl weather, Jimmy.

Bob's heater is electric, snake-tricity. It doesn't warm. I look for liquor, find it, and take a slice of pizza, peeling off the meat—pepperoni was for my kid's sake.

The deer shank's hiding in the way back of the half-sized fridge. Nothing but a hammer to use on the meat so I tenderize with that. I'm browning the meat in onions when Jimmy kindly texts in: *You bring Bob round about my job? Get on with it or get on home, little dogie. You about starving us here.*

No time to text back—and really, who says I want to?— Bob's boots are pounding up the aluminum steps to the door.

"A goddamn out-of-the-blue blizzard," Bob says, shaking snow onto the shag rug. "Should I bring in the dog?"

"Mink's used to being out," I say, stirring, stirring—onions stick.

Bob stuffs a pipe then circles the bowl with a flame. The skunk scent herds off the smell of onions right quick. Bob raises the pipe to my lips and a cold comes off him, a cold that does not stop.

"How'd you learn to cook venison like so?" Bob says, setting down a fork, mouth closing on a burp. We ate like piggy-wiggies, our appetites smoked up.

Bob asks again about the venison. He says, "You cook it like that?" I go ahead then and say what's true about how we all learned the hunt in my family, men and the girls.

He nods, smiles, and that's sweet. He won't mind if I tell him a speck more. "Some of the ladies in my family even been rodeo stars."

"Like who?" Bob says.

I'm about to say how my aunt Debbie was Miss Rodeo America of 1996 but instead I am saying, "Like me."

"Yeah," Bob says.

"Yeah," I say. "I was a big rodeo star, the biggest," I say, only I change the year to be more real. Sometimes the lies come on so fast. I say, "I got into it for the belt buckles."

Bob's nodding that I-know-just-what-you-mean. He says, "You were a real shit kicker."

I keep going on the Aunt Debbie story, making out it is mine, not bothering more with dates. "My daddy bought me a pony the day he got back from Iraq. Called the pony Whinny, like that sound they do. I was just a piddly stable girl, but I got in horsemanship contests and, guess it, I won. Roped good as any cowboy." I am getting carried away, and seeing what was sweet on Bob's face slip off doesn't stop me. I say, "I rope even better when jewelry's involved."

Bob has smoked the last of it. He tongue-taps the lip of the empty bottle. It's a long tongue with a seam up center. He doesn't believe me about the rodeo, but he can't quite finger what's untrue. He slides his legs off the chair then starts working his way through the crap in the tool drawer, the same place I found the hammer to tenderize. He draws out a raw brown rope, a rope that's fraying.

I snatch up the rope and snap it between my hands and get whole puffs of heavy rope dust. The noose I tie I raise above my head and start to twirl. I am my aunt Debbie, Aunt Debbie in stiff denim, hurtling down a lane after a loose pony that someday will not outrun her. When that day comes, Aunt Debbie will have no need of props—for all the ponies will now chase after her. My lasso knocks curtains off rods and flies a dried-out plant from a window ledge.

Bob is not laughing. His long torso tilts so as to pick up the rope from where I dropped it. He says, "Tie me up like you would a *little biddy* spring calf."

As in prayer, he joins his big pink hands at the wrists, except the fingers fold up to fists at my nose. His eyes roll up like a boy pleading to Jesus. I wrap the rope around his wrists, over fast over, hauling rope taut. It hurts and he says so and he lifts a knee and nudges me in the belly. He tells me I stink and the stink has rubbed off on my dog that smells like a kind of stink that's close to human.

Bob raises up the noose on the toe of his boot and says, "Your piggin' string, ma'am."

I shake my head and Bob lowers his boot and steps behind me. The quivering starts in my butt, probably very white under my shorts. Bob's boot is in my back and next thing my face is shoveling the shag rug. Something so tiny drops out my mouth. My tongue checks on each tooth, running along and finding only scum. A horse is sorry for its mouth when Aunt Debbie scrubs those bamboo teeth with a hairbrush for all I could see, horse made to grin until she was done.

Bob's not-so-nimble fingers cannot undo the roping, so he's trying to loosen the binds by striking the heel of his boot at his wrists when I grab hold the trailing end of the rope and give a good yank. Bob rears back and topples onto the floor. Before he knows it—a wrap and a slap—I've got his wrists tied to his ankle, piggin' string. My trusty horse keeps tension on the rope by backing away a smidge, that's all.

"You hoist me about like that?" Bob says. "Twist me flat and that?"

His cow-dumb eyeball swirl-jerks in his skull as I wrap the

last length of rope round his neck. He'd stop choking on his spittle if only he'd relax. I climb up on my mount and straddle the hollow between his hips to gentle him. "I will untie you," I say. "You going to be good so we can do this nice?"

Bob's tongue curls from his mouth. A nod is the best he can do.

I watch him plunge out into tall grass, skipping and rollicking, a newborn calf. Nothing torn, but hear that whinny, that whinny, that whine—it's me, all mine.

Snow bursts in, flakes going to water on my thighs.

Bob lids the pizza box with careful hands then throws it out the door of his home. "Get out," Bob says and he pitches my car keys into the snow.

"Where's Jimmy's money?" I say.

"You smoked it." Bob pushes me into the flurry.

"What am I going to tell Jimmy?"

Bob leans against the doorway, rubbing his blazing red throat. A shiver runs down him until his stomach jerks, like a solid passed through. "Tell him Monday morning he's back on the job. You're welcome." He shuts the door.

Up to this very minute I thought there was some daylight left. Getting down on my knees in the six inches it must have snowed, me, in shorts I would not call hot pants now. I start poking around for the keys, marveling at what a freak weather is. The keys landed on the pizza that's still in the box, but the dough's gone wet. It's one of those snows set to slush.

The trailer park's got some things, like a public restroom with a hand blower. The blower sends good hot air out across the bumps on my legs. The pizza dough gets dry okay under heat. My kid'll never know.

The mirror catches me on the way out. Just straighten up the shoulders, and it's a look but not of failure. I'm going then when I see myself—Jesus, there's nobody else—and I am in one second this piss scared of her—me—the me I must give my hand to—I light out.

The lamp flicks off in Bob's home when I knock on the door. "Bob," I say. "Hello, Bob!"

Scardy-snake slides up to the window where the plant was stood and he thinks only he's seeing me.

"Bob," I say, "Jimmy doesn't want your job." Then this I let him know: "Jimmy's better than that."

And I'm thinking, what is my mouth, what it will say, when all I'm thinking is let him go, let him go?

"Wake up, Mink." I peel off a slice of pizza and set it on the bench seat by his snout. It's hard for him to eat without his full dog's teeth, but pizza makes the difference.

Pretty soon the sound of his jaws mincing meat sends my belly to a place I will not ever make it back from if I keep listening.

What to do is to keep moving. The way this car got parked, nose to a flouncy Noble fur, there's no going forward so I ram the stick in reverse. Wheels spin and spin, the tires gaining no hold on the snow but spraying up slush and splattering the screen. In the rear view something is coming at us full gallop. I throw the car in drive and it smashes into the Noble. Mink tumbles to the floor. I tug the stick into reverse—at least the movement gained us traction—and squint into the rear view, flinching like it will hit. Whatever was in the mirror is retreating now, maybe always was, and next thing I'm backing out, thinking ought I find another way?

SO NOW SORROW

T'S MY P'S AND MY B'S. IT'S HOW I can't write them always in the right place of a word. Words that're using p's and b's I can say. But it's how you're writing that gets their ass up. Teacher's got me putting an up stick on the p's so they'll be b's and putting a down stick on the p's so they'll be etc., and all I'm getting is fucked.

P's may come out like b's when I've got the pen to the paper, but they always snap back into position when I read them back to me. I'm saying I read them just like you read them if you're not so dumb as my sister, Judy, reads them. It's my hand that's doing it. It's doing it when it's got the ben to the paper.

I can say words using the letters but I'm careful. Try saying words with them. They make a mess on the lips. To say the letter b, you've got to get the top and bottom lip up flat against the teeth, then you finish on a pop that blows. P's are the same, but there's that push of air at the top.

"Labials," Teacher says.

I can't fucking believe she says a word like that out loud. There's a lot I can't fucking believe about Teacher.

It's Teacher that keeps keeping me every year. So now sorrow—Judy and I got the same 7th grade. Judy may sit up front at the table with the other dumbs, reading out loud from books with nursery rhymes, but we got the same room. We both got Teacher (let me say here that Teacher, she's okay; we've just seen enough of each other). Now Judy thinks since we got it all the same at school we got to walk home together, too. I tell her I am not walking with a sister who can't keep her shoes tied—one *is* always untied and that's not smart since her shoes are big on her since those very same shoes are the ones that just stopped fitting me. So when she does squat down to tie one, I move ass because Judy's too fat to catch up.

Judy caught up with me yesterday.

"Look out," is what I said to Judy then, and I snapped on her shirt so it ripped all to boobs. She fell on me. I punched her off, but my hand got into fat and when I looked to where my hand had gone, I saw—fat, yeah, but this skin pulling so far across Judy's fat had to hurt. Had to. Anyway, she's doing right getting her skin so fat. It keeps the fucked world out, sending punches faraway into some other body's night.

It's not like I didn't hear about this thing with fat before. It's what kids that got all those pounds do. But it was seeing it in my own sister for a split, seeing wrongly how her fat is right—that's what it was. Sometimes I do see. I see a p standing in for a b. When I see that, I know I'm sick, and something starts growing up out my throat. I press my lips shut.

Teacher's mixing with the dumbs up front now and all the sudden I hear, "What is that?" She's saying it to Judy. She's saying, "There, Judy, there."

It isn't just me heard it. All the good students between me and Judy look up from their chapter's reading on *The Age of Chivalry* to see Judy standing up now and looking all around her fat body for the "there" to what Teacher was referring. Judy doesn't have any idea what Teacher is putting to her even though the black and blue on her upper arm is a jewel.

"There," Teacher points at Judy's arm, "there!!"

Judy still doesn't get it—yeah, she gets that Teacher is making her life a little more up in everyone's fucking face than she'd have it, but she doesn't get what Teacher is pointing at, blacks and blues, and the punches that made them, as much a part of her as fat.

Teacher doesn't get this about Judy, either—getting it would be low, like be*low* her to think of some people living a life receiving punches regular as mail—so she keeps asking Judy, "Did you, Judy, fall down or something?"

All the good students in the room are coming to life now. That's not the first black and blue to show up on Judy. How fucking blind can Teacher be?!

"This is something," Teacher says. "You mustn't be afraid to talk."

Don't you say a fucking word, I say with my eyes to Judy. I keep looking at her like, so hard, she'll go up in fire, she'll go boil under the hairs that'll short and the skin, that'll go black, and it'll buckle back and back and . . . all the sudden, at this very moment, I'm sick. That something has already started growing up out of my throat. So what I do is swallow, big, to hold it back. All this does is make *a noise*—and fuck what—the noise sounds just like Old Dad's pipe playing, ploob-ploop-plumb.

Let me explain something here: me and Judy got Old Dad. Old Dad talks two ways. He talks with the palm of his hand (meaning you are fucked), but he talks with the seat of his pants, too (meaning you are in for laughs).

Low is what Teacher would call Old Dad's pant-seat talk. Lowness doesn't stop Old Dad though. Just anywhere, at the dinner table even, his pant-seat will start piping, ploob-ploop-plumb. Sure, Old Dad's just slicing farts, but the thing is you got to laugh, got to.

Judy doesn't. She doesn't get that it's Old Dad blaying the pipe, so she doesn't laugh, and for that she gets the palm of his hand.

This Old Dad, he plays one, he plays nick-knack on my thumb, with a nick-knack, paddy-whack . . .

Judy's still up front with the dumbs and the biggest fucking dumb of them all, Teacher, who's pointing, saying, "Somebody laid a hand on you, didn't they?"

I got to do something about Teacher.

"Who hurt you?"

I got to explain about Judy before it's everyone's fucking business.

I start writing it down.

"Excuse me, Teacher." I stand up with what I wrote and I say, "I got something here for you to read." Teacher takes the paper. But she doesn't look it over to herself then fold it up and put it away in the pocket of her dress. What she does is read this what I wrote to explain about Judy. What I'm telling you is she reads it out loud.

Teacher reads: "When Old Dad took us to cages with baby baboons and daddy baboons—their dicky-things thinner than the thump on your hand—those daddy papoons grapping at papoon girl papies, and the girl papies screaming and pappling so much the peasts in other cages got whibbed ub to a papple, and Old Dad and us are laughing, put Judy, she starts ub the pappling, too, and Old Dad makes to shut her ub with a punch, pam-pam!! He hits skin, then pone, and snab, maype a pone preak."

I shut my mouth because, I can tell you, it had come open.

You know what happens next in a room of dumbs and good students where somebody has written something so wrongly. It's quiet for a mouse and then the laughs come, even Teacher—she's not laughing, okay, but she's stopped messing with Judy so as to sit down and take a look around at the shit she's given such a good stir to. That's okay with me because I got her off Judy's placks and plues, but what's not okay is there's Judy—she's laughing, too.

Judy is laughing at me.

This is news! Judy caught the laughing wind for the first time in her *low* fucking life. What is funny is a bitch to learn. Some never get it, but there's my sister waking up all the sudden to it. Teacher's a genius. She's taught Judy to laugh and to laugh especially at her sister when her sister shows she's near as dumb as her when it comes to using fucking p's and fucking b's.

I got more news for Judy. She may know a punch when she gets one, but the one I'm going to give her for laughing at me will bump her out of this grade, my life, permanent.

I'm marching, left-right, up to the front, where all the dumbs are holding their breath because Teacher is having such a time. And here comes Judy, walking straight to me and scared as fuck. She's not laughing now.

Come on, Judy. My arms are humming-live currents down to hot dongs in my fists.

I know the secret. Judy's got fat to keep punches from hurting. Fat's a metal suit, like those Chivalries put on to bend swords away from the sorrow in their hearts (that's what the book says, *sorrow*). Judy's fat is sword bending—unless you got the right sword. Knowing is a sword, the right sword. What *I know* about Judy's fat will render it a metal suit to everyone, but me. When I punch, my punch will go in, past her fat, to her heart. It's going to do what nobody can do—not Old Dad, either—and that's make Judy sorrow.

Judy knows it. I'm setting her up for my punch when she starts dancing, this way and that. Next thing, her untied shoe comes off. This shoe is all I can get of Judy before she runs back to Teacher.

Teacher doesn't like it, doesn't like how I'm handling my sister in a way that makes shoes come off. She holds Judy's soft shoulders up close against her.

All I got is Judy's shoe.

I'll put it back on her.

I'm down at Judy's feet now, slipping the shoe back on her fat foot, so gentle, oh good sister. But she's not having it. She goes dancing again, trying to get loose from my oh-so-good-sister hands.

All around the mulberry bush—

"Stay still, Judy," says Teacher. "Really, Judy." Judy's even getting to Teacher.

—the monkey chased the weasel.

I look up at Teacher and give the wide eyes, like I'm just trying to help. She buys it because I see her hands, how they go looser on Judy's soft shoulders.

The monkey thought 'twas all in fun . . .

I get Judy's shoe that's too big back on her foot and I tie it up, all ready to put my punch into the laughing fat fuck.

Then POP!

I don't get my chance. But Judy gets in hers—she kicks me. Okay, she misses, but there goes her shoe flying out across the room until it clips a dumb sharp on the head. The dumb starts bawling.

"Christ, Judy," Teacher says, "that was nasty!" Next thing, Teacher's hauling Judy up against the blackboard. Chalk so powders Judy's head, Judy gets to choking on the stuff. It's the only other sound than the sound of Teacher slapping on her. Everything else is just us, quiet.

The whole thing's only so long as it takes. Teacher's just finishing up Judy when the principal charges in. He's got two guys from upper grades with him. He uses them to take Teacher out.

The way she says good-bye to us, the way her waving hand looks—red from all the slapping—tells me Teacher won't be around to keep keeping me back anymore.

Old Dad's supposed to pick Judy and me up from the principal's office. We got to wait if it takes all night. But the principal's not waiting all night so Judy and me go ahead and walk home together. I might've made it before dark but for waiting on Judy to tie her fucking shoes.

THE WAY OF AFFLICTION

THE CHILDREN THESE BEDS HOLD. LITTLE ONES WITH broken legs or bellies swelled on household cleaners. Flu, a spoiled food, a hand laid too hard, could be collision, undertow, burn, could be a million so many things that send a child in. When she thinks of the well of hurts a child can fall into, when she thinks. It is better not to think.

She shakes out the sheet, flying it over the small mattress: a toddler with a rattlesnake bite and a baby with a gunshot wound just ambulance rides away. Blaring through LA traffic on a Friday afternoon, up Vermont Avenue, any minute the ambulances will roll in, the teams wheeling into the pediatric ICU to pull up gurneys alongside these beds. On the corner of the mattress, she bends and tucks, wrenching her leg.

"Irina," Nurse Garland says. "Take the snakebite."

No, you take the snakebite, she wants to say. By all means. But she can't risk it. They've given her one final chance.

"Jen's on the gunshot. The rest of us are out at nine." Garland's crooked forefinger and thumb flick the top sheet, testing. "You can lose children on loose sheets."

Whatever they throw at her, Irina knows how to make tight a bed. When she reported for work this afternoon, Garland said she'd gone out on a limb for Irina. So Irina filled out the time card, found a locker, pulled on scrubs. No questions. No more screw-ups. You play your part.

Garland nods at Irina and saunters out, teddy bear print smock inching up her scrubs.

The joggling of gurney wheels, the rush of feet, the medics calling out, nurse, intake, uptake, blood pressure, the sound dins in Irina's ears like the thump of Mamochka's broom on the ceiling, they were all tumbling into ICU now. She turns from the bed and is met by a shock of undefended blue. The mother's eyes plead with Irina to make her child right again as she clings to a small, limp hand.

Irina says to the medic, "Where was bite?"

Instead of answering, the medic draws the transport sheet off the child's bony leg and, with shaky hands, lifts it up. Two puncture marks gape above the soft knob of the ankle. Irina's own leg almost buckles under her.

"Hello? Irina, care to pitch in?"

Irina bobs her head at Garland. Three sets of hands, including hers now, shift the child onto the bed she has made. Notations on the venom's progress have been written directly onto the child's milk-white skin. But the venom creeps up the artery, overtaking each mark of the pen.

Like a nestling pinned by a predator, the girl's hazel eyes scan the faces of the people attending her. She pants.

"Is all this necessary?" the mother says. "She was fine before."

Before what? The child is naked. She must wear a diaper. She must wear a shirt to keep her chest warm. She must get between clean tight sheets. She must take the anti-venin in one arm. She must take the saline drip in another. She must take the IV of Fentanyl and Versed. Look at her, lady. You think she can't use the forgetting?

A doctor Irina has not worked with before breaks from a group of white coats he's been consulting and steps into the room. "I am Dr. Alvaro," he says, his head of black slickened hair just reaching the mother's shoulder. "I will be the presiding doctor. I understand that it was a rattlesnake that bit Gemma? You are sure of this?"

"Do we have to do this again?" the mother says.

The husband explains that they went over the particulars with the poison expert in admittance, that rattlesnakes congregate on his low-mountain property, that they heard the rattle, saw black skin, scales shaped in diamonds—

"Gemma is currently receiving her second vial of anti-venin." Alvaro is moving on.

"Once that kicks in," the mother tells her husband, "it'll be okay."

"We are contacting other hospitals for additional vials," Alvaro says.

"Why?"

"Anti-venin is unstable. No hospital stores more than a few."

"No, I mean, she's a little girl. How much can she need?" The mother wraps herself in her own arms. Her teeth clatter, a quiet sound but no mistaking it.

"Nurse," Dr. Alvaro says, eyes on the mother.

Irina steps up to the woman. "You're afraid," she whispers. "Do not let the child see."

The mother's eyes go wide. "Thank you. I think I know how I feel, Nurse." She yanks on the strap of her white shoulder bag and whirls away, slamming straight into a wall.

The second patient has arrived, a baby swathed in bandaging where a bullet lodged in his cheek. The child's parents are not welcome into the examination room. Outside the child's door, the two sit close, his brown arms folded over hers the way only young people do.

Striding through the nurses' station is Garland, trailed by a couple of police officers. She claps her hands at the young parents—as though their downcast eyes were indication of inattention. "These gentleman would like a word with you."

The young mother will not return Irina's smile as she precedes the officers into a back room, the last officer shutting the door. Then from behind a dividing curtain, in totemic procession, two nurses glide out, arms bent, palms rolling little glass vials as if sifting gold or sparking willow. So careful you think nitroglycerin.

"What this?" Irina says.

"Anti-venin," one says. "It mixes from just the heat of our hands."

The radiance of the vials reminds Irina of the winter sun flaring in the bottles that Mamochka stacked against the windows of their logged home. Sun stored in a bottle. Don't do it. Don't go back, not for a second. You're here now.

"You see the mother's face?" one nurse says.

"What do you want?" says the other. "A snake bit her kid!"

Sympathy is pouring like syrup. Talk about accident, snakebite is an accident. The baby with a gunshot wound? Not a word about him or his parents. Nobody likes cops' leathers creaking through ICU. Lowers morale. Where were Mom and Pop when the gun went off anyway? Give her the young Latino couple any day. They keep the pain to themselves. The baby has a better chance when the parents don't give in to sentiment. That child with venom winding to her heart needs her mother's strength. It takes discipline to love hard, like Mamochka.

Snow pressed at the glass when Mamochka forgot to close the shutters, tucking them in great white sheets. Hoping the snow would pile up to the roof, Irina rapped her knuckles in time to the high gurgling *toc-toc* of the raven circling in the upper panes. This snakebite has set her mind off—set her leg off, too. Won't it do that, act up, out of the blue? The child's leg, her leg, how can she not feel it? Coincidence is all that brought them here, nothing more. Best keep it at that if she's to make good on the job.

Irina pulls an ice pack from the freezer, feeling Garland's watchful eye. "The next vial's almost set," Garland says. "Check the IV." On entering the patient's room, Irina hands the ice pack to the husband, glancing at the mother. The mother glares back.

The husband sets the ice pack against his wife's forehead, still red from hitting the wall. His wife knocks the ice pack aside then leans across her child to adjust the sheet. The mother's tie-dyed yoga pants are beginning to sag at her toned hips. Soon she will look for someone to blame. A rattlesnake biting a child is terrible, no denying it. But what does this pampered woman know of nature's cruelties? Deceiving herself about the child's condition is a temporary fix. Best stay on guard, someone must be held to account for this terrible strike of misfortune, and it might just be you.

Irina works her way around the bed to check the drip. The mother's roomy handbag open at the foot of the bed trips her—stupid leg—and she grabs the backboard to break her fall. She reaches for the handbag to store it on a shelf when something long and gray pours over the white lip like fluid muscle. The handbag drops, scales in patterns of black on white slipping out. Just when she thinks the thing will never stop coming, it winds up in adjacent rows of translucent honeycomb.

Her feet adhere to the floor, legs seized up and gone fluid. When someone points, she realizes it's her hand.

"What?" The father stares at Irina. "What is it? Gemma?"

Irina looks back at the handbag, but the snake is gone. Her heart rushes at her ribs. A snake? Here, in hospital? Impossible. But what had she seen if not that? She squints at the father. Is it right to alarm him? He returns her gaze with dull eyes then goes back to bemoaning the hospital's scant choice of children's movies.

"Gemma is not watching a movie," his wife tells him. "Our family is media free."

Irina backs out of the room, scanning the corners.

Coming after her is Doctor Alvaro, supplying instructions on the drip rate of the anti-venin, reminding her to mark the poison's progress up the leg. "I'm going now," he says. "Make sure to monitor pain levels closely. Contact me if you become concerned."

"Dr. Alvaro, there is snake," Irina blurts but it comes out a whisper.

"Yes there was a snake."

"No, snake is in there." Her eyes jump to the room then back to him.

The doctor's eyebrows slide together as he looks at Irina, really looks, actually sees her—though her good looks are startling, he does not appear a connoisseur. He exhales out his small mouth. "What is your accent? Russian?"

"I am born in Siberia," she says.

"They see snakes in hospitals in Siberia?" He smiles and reminds her it will be a long night. Excusing himself, he strides over to Garland.

Through the viewing window, the mother motions to her. Irina steps up to the door, hesitates—please no snake. Luckily, Alvaro thought it was a joke. Really, she didn't believe it either. Gemma's shining rheumy eyes follow her around the bed as she sweeps the room for a sign. How foolish. The child, those ashy curls at her temple, she is her concern, not some snake that doesn't exist.

"What about for pain?" the mother says.

"Versed." Irina indicates the drip. "She will be complete out of pain." She is quoting Dr. Alvaro here.

"Versed?"

"No, is Ver*sed,* like unfed. Is drug that induces amnesia during time she's receive it."

"Isn't that dandy?" The mother looks sideways at her husband. "She won't remember any of this."

That's right. Don't you believe. There's no forgetting. Take Irina. She perched above a sea of snow. The wind had shaped waves, cresting at her feet. Four of them hoop hollering on the rooftop, felt boots stomping. Any kid in her right mind would jump. Let snow catch you. Bang bang. *Off my roof, hooligans.* Mamochka's broom thumps the ceiling under your boots. *Toc-toc,* the raven over your heads blotches the sky. Bang bang. *Criminals!* A sheet chunks off and huffs down the roof. No one wants to jump first. Cowards. Devil take you. You jump. Now the others do, too. Whoop, whoop, whoop, white swallows all. Howls of fright—but you do not cry out from the pain. Mamochka would snap your neck if you made a racket. Keep your mouth shut no matter how bad.

"I *want* her to remember," the mother says. "I mean, remember the normal stuff. Honey, make yourself useful? Get my little photo album."

"Gemma's not capable of taking in anything right now," the husband says.

"You don't know that," she says. "The pictures are in my purse."

The mother's handbag is where Irina dropped it, surfacing from under the bed. Irina leans over, hesitating at the winding strap. Don't be an idiot. She grabs it and swings it over—the mother suddenly beside her—and accidentally slugs her.

They both gasp.

"I am sorry," Irina says. "I did not—"

"I love being hit with my own purse," the mother says. Her hands dive into the gaping white leather. Irina cannot watch.

"See the baby, Gemma?" The mother croons over the album. "That's you!" As Irina heads for the door, she glimpses a snapshot of the mother's wide smile of surrender as she suds her baby in a bubble bath.

The nurses' station is quiet. A cup of instant soup scrounged from the kitchenette rotates in the microwave. Irina presses her palm against the tinted door to prop herself up. She imagines Mamochka looking at that mother's photo album, her tongue clucking, indulgently, but the blacks of her eyes are points of contempt. Why make bubbles of a child when a soap bar will do the job? Irina conjures her own childhood photo album, which neither she nor anyone else had, one photograph after another of only her leg, knobby and bruised, like any child's, soaking in bubbles that rise in airy prisms of white, buoying and building up the leg until it is healed. Now the leg leaps like a hare out of the white.

The microwave beeps. Nurse Garland's reflection flashes as Irina swings open the microwave door. But when she turns around, it's just Garland's back retreating down the hallway. Irina hurries with her soup to the nurses' station. In the next moment, Gemma's father slogs up, buttoning a professorial sweater beneath the gray weight of his face. He asks if he might lie down. "There's a couch you can," says Nurse Jen.

The buzzer lights up. Couldn't she wait ten minutes when Irina will do her rounds?

"She's cold," the mother says, caressing her child's cheek. In an apparent effort to shield her child, she has gotten into the bed with Gemma. What does this woman think she is, Mother Teresa?

"Is because diaper is wet." Irina removes the diaper, sodden with fluid from the drip. The child's flaking skin is rough yet silvery, like the bark of a winter tree.

The mother scrutinizes Irina as she eases a fresh one under the child, who lifts up a little to assist. "Gemma likes us to sing to her at changing time," she says.

Irina isn't sure who's supposed to sing. Her? The mother?

"No, no, but that's way too tight." The mother undoes Irina's work and commences the diapering from scratch. All at once Gemma moans. No whimpering, bawling, crying out, the child can't seem to spare a tear. She just moans.

"Why is she doing that?"

Because you vex everything, even a diapering, Irina wants to say. Instead she dials up the pain drip, enough for sleep. "She will stop." The shadow of the IV line quivers against the wall. Don't be a fool. Everything is not a snake. But she scans the room to make sure. Noticing the discarded photo album, she brings it to the mother, but the mother has already shoved a DVD into the player.

On her way to the door Irina pauses by a fine woven sweater tossed onto a chair. The mother is the one who's cold. She could bring it to her. Not such a grand gesture. Irina picks up the sweater, but a button catches on the heavy-duty fabric of the cushion and now instead of sweater, it's chair screeching toward her. Under the chair a sound shoots like water through a rotor head. A garden sprinkler in here? That's no sprinkler. Not that she's heard a snake's rattle before, but there's no mistaking *this*. She gapes at the mother, who turns up the volume on the TV monitor. Irina lets go the sweater. The rattling stops.

Jen is not in the nurses' station so Irina legs it to the gunshot baby's room, toe banging the door in her rush. She tries not to shout. "Nurse Jen, you must to come. I heard it—"

But the room is empty except for the baby with the placid bandage across his cheek. All at once a head pops up from behind the crib, Nurse Jen, face a grimace. Pinched between her fingers is a dangling wisp. "Look, Irina, snakeskin!"

It's true. Snakes shed skin. It must have shed in here. The colorless husk is proof! You're not losing it. You're not alone. You could kiss Jen.

"Eeew, catch." Jen flings the skin at her.

Irina flinches so the skin bumps her cheek then floats down and drapes across her white leather shoe, nothing but a strip of surgical gauze, not snakeskin at all.

"I heard you tell Alvaro you saw a snake," Jen says, the eyes of her muffin face bursts of joy. "What if Garland had heard you?"

Irina shrugs. "She has no sense of humor."

"Seriously!" Jen scoots around the crib, calling on her way out, "You hungry?"

If only the snake were a joke played by a nurse. But that is never the way of affliction. From her old world to the new, she carries the affliction in her leg that won't mend. Such weakness attracts things like snakes. Is that why the mother brought it in, to remind Gemma that she, too, can never be safe again? Which is not to say that the mother meant to take the snake along, but plainly she left her handbag open.

Scales of wax from the cup lining float on the surface of Irina's soup. Not that she has any appetite. Best keep focused on the things in front of you, the clock, the monitor, the chart, and keep your mind on the work, the forms to fill out, the rounds left to do. Show Garland you can do your job.

The microwave hums, burnt tomato sauce stinking the nurses' station. Jen ambles out the kitchen, pushing a plastic utensil through spaghetti steaming from a Styrofoam bowl. Her rump drops on the edge of the desk as her small front teeth break off the gleaming noodles. "You're fun," she says. "Have we worked together before?"

Irina blinks at Jen. "What?"

"No, I mean, like you on day shift? I'm on nights. Yeah, nights and nights." Jen wipes the edges of the Styrofoam with stale bread Irina recognizes from the cafeteria—a rattlesnake in the pediatric ICU and she's identifying stale bread. The mind doesn't want to know. Stop. There's no snake in here, and thank God. Otherwise she'd have to sound the alarm. Call plant operations. Or did firemen remove snakes? Just what she needed. Her first time back, and she's causing a panic.

Jen forks up spaghetti and pushes it into her mouth. Another bite fast on the other, slurping noodles. Jen sees Irina see her and reddens.

"It's yummy, yeah?" Irina says gently and smiles.

After a moment Jen smiles back then stares down at her bowl. "Did you hurt your leg . . . I saw how you kind of were limping? Are you like on probation—sorry, that's just what someone said."

The buzzer goes off again at the nurses' station. Behind the viewing glass, the mother's silhouette looms. Just after 4 a.m. and the mother stares at the TV monitor propped on the overbed table. Worn to threads by lack of sleep, she cradles her child's small head that moves steadily side to side, as if in continual rejection of both the pain and the needles that convey relief. Optimism can no longer insulate the mother from the glaze of terror in Gemma's eyes.

"How did it happen?" Irina says. "How could snake bite this child?"

The mother's blanched eyes narrow at Irina. She regards her for a moment. "Gemma ran in the grass outside our house. Past where it must of, um, must of coiled. If it rattled . . . that's not something intelligible, like a shout or something, I mean, the snake bit."

"Like that, no warning?"

"I know, right? I always thought of rattlesnakes as gentleman. They don't strike first. They rattle as a courtesy."

"You sing to her, yes? What is it you sing?"

"She can't sleep. Her leg," the mother says, her attention now on the child who has started to moan again, "should it be so painful?"

Irina lifts the bed sheet. In spite of the infusion of anti-venin, the poison advances. The puncture marks on the swollen ankle seem to stare at her. Was edema in evidence earlier? "Alvaro said this is expected for now."

"That's not what *I* expected. The anti-venin was supposed to work. We want to go home. Back to normal."

So unaccustomed to suffering, this woman of yoga pants who contorts the body to feel good. "Pain medication is at maximum levels," Irina says. "I cannot increase."

"Ah, okay. Now how about a little compassion, lady? She hurts—"

"Sure, she hurts." Irina gestures at a rattlesnake that isn't there, that she hopes isn't there. "Snake bite her. Children are in pain. They survive."

The mother gapes at her. "You're way out of line," she says. "Where do you get off?"

Irina does not know where she gets off. It is true that those words came out of her, but they were not really hers. They were something Mamochka would say. Perhaps it does seem hard. But that is how it is to survive. Irina shrugs and withdraws from the room.

The nurses' station is unoccupied. Jen probably snuck off to eat. If the nurse offered some morsel to stopper the hurt, Irina would not refuse. The pain creeps up. Before you know it, you let loose on somebody, like that mother. She's torn up about her kid. Why go at her like that? Wasn't Gemma's accident bad enough? The thoughts run through Irina's mind, and suddenly she has an image of the mother as a little girl wading into a brook. Turtles glide through her palms to peekaboo between her fingers. Woodland creatures line the banks with ferns to pat dry her legs, while a raven sings to her and a snake is a gentleman. She thinks of Gemma's mouth on the mother's breast. She thinks of the mother cradling her child, promising a world where all creatures pledge to keep her safe. It occurs to Irina that when the mother left open her handbag, it was innocently done.

The buzzer goes off. "Call the doctor, Nurse!" The door barely muffles the mother's shouts. "Call Dr. Alvaro!"

Irina looks at her watch. Alvaro is due in two hours. It's better the doctor gets sleep. He will need it to handle this mother. Irina would go to the mother if only her own leg didn't hurt.

A landscape of white. Red and blue knitted caps buoyed up by the snow. One boy howled at Irina's blood dotting the snow. Shinbone snapped, white bone poked through her skin. How could you let out such a ragged thing? Mamochka hollering at the children, swiping her broom until they scattered best they might in the high high snow. Irina knew better than to cry when Mamochka hoisted her onto a mended wooden sled. The snow pushed through the slats, but she didn't mind. She was hot. Then she was cold and began to shiver, but the blanket wrapped around her was caving under the snow. She dare not adjust it. What if the sled tipped? It barely held now.

"You pant like an animal," Mamochka said. "Be quiet."

The snowflakes fell in wet leaves, soaking the dressing on her leg, the bone jutting through like a tooth. Her mother's back a narrow point in the woolen coat. The snow crouched beneath the blades of the sled, each jerk and pull jostling the bone, steady steady jabs, endurable, reliable. Once in a while a working light swung from the wires above, creaking. Bang! All at once the sled overturned. She tasted vomit as Mamochka wiped her mouth with the blanket and said, "You are weak. The weak do not survive."

That old injury has you in its spell. Down and down you go. Round and round you go. A tune playing on someone's hand-held device drifts on the hallway. All else is quiet in the ICU except for the moaning of a child. She enters Gemma's room to find the mother's head sunk to her shoulder. But her child does not sleep. Gemma's mouth hangs open as she stares at the rattlesnake coiled beside her mother's handbag at the foot of the bed. The snake's mouth unlocks, the tips of the fangs dangling balls of buttery venom.

How could she forget about the snake? Such negligence!

"Be gone, Affliction!" Irina lunges, knocking the bedstead. The tail switches up and the beads rattle. Oh, how they rattle. Perhaps the snake regrets his earlier discourtesy and wants to make amends. He will keep the child safe now, like a little mother.

A song Mamochka might have sung rises in Irina's throat. The lullaby gives her courage as she reaches for the strap. As if he understands, the snake unwinds and slips back into the handbag. Irina can hardly believe it. This horrible gift. Gingerly she draws the handbag up by the strap. Closing the front flap, she ensnares the snake.

The mother's head jerks upright. She blinks at Irina in confusion. "What are you doing? Ah, that's . . . that's my bag."

"Shhh." Irina backs away with the handbag. "Is okay. I got it."

"Give me my bag." The mother yanks off the tucked sheets, only to become entangled in the tubes running into Gemma. Irina whirls round to the door, but the mother intercepts. Catching hold of the strap, she hauls back on it, throwing Irina off balance. Irina's leg gives out and she drops to the floor, clinging still to the bag.

"You okay?" the mother says.

"Is nothing." Irina pushes up to sitting, which takes some time. She uses the arm of the chair for leverage but can't take the pressure on her leg and drops back to the floor.

The mother squats beside Irina, placing a hand on her shin. "Is it your leg?"

Irina shrugs. "It is mine." She pats the handbag. "Snake is yours. You are lucky. It is in here."

The mother looks at her handbag, starting a smile. "There's a snake in my purse?"

"He is gentleman, really," Irina says. Thinking of the mother's promise to her baby, she hands up the purse. "Go on. Is for you to take out of here."

The mother stares at the handbag. Even as Nurse Garland pushes in at the door, accidentally banging Irina's leg, the mother just stares.

Garland assesses the scene. "What the hell did you do now, Irina?"

The mother's head slowly turns toward Garland. Her eyes rake down the woman. "Irina was trying to protect us," she says, reaching for her handbag at last. Holding it by the strap, extended from her body, she throws a glance at Irina and walks the hand bag out of the room.

DEAF DOG

THIS DEAF DOG WITH LIMITED VISION CAN LEARN hand signals is how the ad goes. It goes like this—take Tiny home, give him a home, hold out your hand, point, just point, don't call, Tiny, Tiny—remember Tiny's deaf. Signal to Tiny, signal in bright light. Get his attention by holding him—he fits in one hand. Tiny weighs less than a shoe.

A big dog is more what I'm interested in. I didn't know this until I saw what was available, saw this dog with such limits, this little dog nobody wants. I can see not wanting a little dog. Little ones bark.

Maybe this Tiny could be a quiet dog, being a deaf. My landlady likes quiet. "Those sounds I hear coming from your place," she says. "I don't want to."

That bit about hand signals—I don't see making out with my hands. Besides, there's the situation with the light in my place. It might make hand signals hard for Tiny to see. By the pool I could work a few things with him, out in sunshine. A leash would keep him clear of suntanners. Tiny can still smell, right? Nothing here about loss of smell. Those sun-tanners rub up their skin with sweet oil that does attract.

The ad says Tiny can fit in your hand. It says Tiny weighs less than a shoe—but can he squeeze into one? I might have just the shoe for Tiny. It's still new, since I stopped wearing it. My landlady knows about that, about why I stopped wearing new shoes.

"We have services here," she told me when I applied to rent the place.

"Do you polish shoes?" I said.

"Sure," she said, "and we help you tie them, too."

No other tenants had placed shoes out on the welcome mats. I set out my pair, and in the morning one shoe was gone.

My landlady would have noticed the quality. My landlady and I are about the same size. We could have the same shoe size. She could have taken a shoe. I don't know why.

Here is an advantage to Tiny over a big dog—Tiny could sleep in my shoe that doesn't have a mate. The sides of the shoe keep the foot snug. I could lace Tiny in. What a comfort it might be to this little deaf dog, what a dear.

No pets allowed. My landlady said it from the start, but I think she just said that to me. She doesn't want me to have anybody. People have pets here. You can smell pets on their skin. If I get a big, good-looking dog, that would say I can have somebody, too. Tiny is saying it under your tongue.

Maybe that's the way to say it to my landlady.

Last week is when this ad is dated. Tiny could be adopted. Little ones do go fast. Tiny has a lot to offer—maybe he can't hear, but that can be an advantage. People think it's loud sounds that drive you out of your place, but it's the slight bit pinning at the rim of your ear. Shoe creaks, her breathing in, breathing out, all that gets you feeling antsy.

Tiny's limited vision takes extra thought. Day for him may be like night, like my nights lit only with pool light wavy on my bedroom wall. I suppose you can get used to limited vision if it's anything like limited light. Light isn't coming from inside your home or, as in Tiny's case, from inside the part of the eye that makes light. Limited might just mean limited by how much things around you shed light.

It's easy to see my landlady looking inside my window at night since my rooms are pretty much dark. She's trying to drive me out, but she'll have to catch me at something first. She thought she had me when I stopped paying the electric, but I make the rent. As long as I do, it'll stay my place, a home to put Tiny in.

Now if Tiny's not little enough to sleep in my shoe, he can sleep in my bed. He might pillow into the empty pillow next to mine or tuck into the nook between my chin and collar bone. He might even line along the small of my back. I'd try to discourage that—Tiny is something easily crushed.

If Tiny's fur is good, I might sleep naked for that. Tiny will like my breasts. Little things never lose a feeling for nipples. Some people may think that's unnatural, but dogs don't worry about what people think. To dogs the world is available, without limits.

Others might see Tiny as limited—I may have at first—but this is not how Tiny sees himself. I once saw a dog with a crippled back leg that was running along like he still had four good legs. Dogs need to get around. That's what they do. In a way, a dog is just another verb for run. Being three-legged, deaf, limited in vision—that's not going to stop a dog. It goes like this—limitations in the body only ramp up a dog's drive to get around. I read that dogs stick their heads out car windows to 'simulate running.' There it is—a dog locked inside a moving car still needs to get around even if only his head can. If all a dog had for a body was a head, he'd open and close his jaws to keep going. People may not understand this, and really, otherwise they'd think twice about those carts they construct to strap in dogs whose back legs are no good. All those carts do is make life easier for people who can't look at limitations. But the dog that's getting around by dragging one, two, even three no-good legs after him doesn't mind—he's going. He may even go in a way that beats the devil out of other dogs with four good legs. Running isn't the only way of getting around. Dogs can go pretty far on a good bark, a bark that scares. If a dog with only one leg has a bark that makes other dogs run away, then he's gotten around, hasn't he?

Maybe Tiny is not a barker, but her sniffer still works, doesn't it? Odds are that her nose is what she uses to get around—even if a nose is the most leathered and least alive-seeming part of a dog's face. It's other people's problem to feel sick at the sight of Tiny over-working her nose—Tiny's not bothered.

That time I pulled on a bathing suit and took a dip in the pool, my landlady said, "Do you have to twist your hips around like that?" Just the sight of me made her sick.

I said, "If I want to get to the other side."

"Stay out," she said. "Nobody likes to think you might be drowning."

Then this is what she did—she looked at my *breasts* in my bathing suit. Maybe she didn't want to but she looked.

Would she ever say she looked? Whatever it is in my land lady that's sick at the sight of me over-working my hips in the pool but will stop to look at my breasts might be the least alive-seeming part of her, but it's the part she uses to get around.

I can't take Tiny home, I can't give her a home. Tiny's deaf but this is not why. Either is her limited vision. Tiny isn't limited by any of this. It's my landlady who's limited. Yes, even a big, good-looking girl like her has limits. Being this kind of girl, she wants to get in, into my place, into my bathing suit. For making her want to get in, for this, she *must* drive me out. It's not her fault how little the things around her shed light. She has her limits. No dogs allowed, she said, and she'll hold to it. My landlady's my limit. She's mine.

ANIMAL CONTROL

NO ONE'S BEEN BITTEN. NO LAWNS DIRTIED. NO one's even seen one. But the house has begun to smell. You can smell it from the street.

"Keeps them locked inside," says a man holding a child's backpack. He watches from his driveway as I approach the house. "Give my neighbor a good knock."

He means the door, of course, a good knock on his neighbor's door, which is my intention. However before making contact, I like to review the Rules of Procedural Policy. Follow these and everything stays under control. Number one, register all complaints (check). Number two, question complainants for just cause (check). Number three, investigate site for possible occupation of domestic animals in excess of code.

I evaluate the externals. Landscaping kept up, minimum peeling paint, sinuous eave intact above the front door. The house is what those in the business call a starter, a couple's first home. Usually the first baby's born here and not long after the couple moves out due to space issues. What those in the business don't mention is sometimes the couple's finished long before a baby's born. In my case, there was a baby. But it's not the look of this house that concerns me. It's the smell.

I knock on the front door. "Hello?" I say, "Anybody home?"

Barks blast from inside. The front door shudders from collected canines hurling against it. I cover my ears, standard procedure. More typical, of course, is cat collecting. People miscalculate the degree of feline unfriendliness and, especially if housebound or forgotten by friends and family, will take in one after another in the misapprehension that the more cats you have the less you will feel the indifference of the world.

I knock again, a *good* knock. A little door set inside the front door opens at eye level. I had not previously noted this little door and now am on guard. "Precinct Manager Deedra Stero, East Valley Animal Control." I put my badge to the screen of the little door.

The individual says something inaudible in response.

"You'll have to quiet them," I shout. Quieting dogs takes time so I turn to face Pleasant Street. On the opposite side is the Chrysalis Preschool. Naptime over, children scuff past their teacher through the bright painted door. One little girl stops to braid her hair. When I noticed on the requisition that this house was on Pleasant Street, I was reluctant to take the call. But Pedro was on assignment for our supervisor, so that left only me to respond.

An audible reduction has been made in barking levels, demonstrating cooperation on the part of the individual inside. I turn back to the house.

Enter site in question only upon notification of headquarters, rule number four. I get Pedro on the line. "Requesting permission to enter."

"What your eval?" Pedro says. "Need back up? Cages? Prods?" When I don't answer, he says, "Nobody was here when I get back, except Goose in sanitation. He say you took a code 5844 on Pleasant Street. You don't take calls on Pleasant Street."

"What were my options? The complainant threatened to call another precinct."

"You near that preschool?"

One more child trudges off with her mother. Letting loose a big yawn, the teacher scans the empty playground then strolls back inside. I don't recognize her. She must be new, like the high fence securing the preschool. "No preschool in sight," I say then get off the line and turn back to the front door. Just then it opens and I am hit with it, like when you lift a lid off banked garbage. An individual, tall, fit, clothed in denim and lace stands in the doorway. "The neighbors are concerned," I say.

"That's awful nice." Though it could go either way, I will identify him as male.

"Their concern is with the smell. *My* concern," I say, "is with the welfare of the dogs."

He opens the door wider and extends a hand, a welcoming hand. "See for yourself," a smile, "if you can stand the smell." His ponytail sweeps side to side as he inhales the air.

Covering my nose as if to sneeze I say, "According to county records, a person by the name of J.J. applied for a dog license at this address. Is that you?"

When he nods, I say, "How should I call you?"

"J.J.'s good."

"J.J.," I say, walking across the threshold into his house. With a brief touch at my shoulder, J.J. directs me down a hallway deep and tunnel-dark. Flies list overhead. Off the hallway, windows blush behind pink sheets. I reach for the wall to brace myself and hear the faint but steady slow pant of dogs. It's coming from behind a closed door, the type that leads to basements, which are atypical in these ranch-style homes. "The dogs down there?"

J.J.'s hand comes up and pats mine, which is also a kind of patting of the doorframe upon which it rests. "Out of harm's way," he says.

J.J. continues down the hallway. When he reaches the kitchen door, he turns to me with another smile. This time I smile back. I excel at sitting down with these people and having a heart-to-heart. "Thank you for allowing me into your home, J.J.," I say. That's rule number five, conduct oneself without judgment. This is key. The process is impersonal. Take J.J. Though he is wide through the hips, he is broad featured and the body is muscular. He is . . . what? Oh, why do people muddy the water? J.J. is male, and I will conduct myself in accordance with my initial ascertainment.

J.J. offers a chair, which is situated beneath a dust-coated skylight. On the table silk roses perk from a pickle jar set down on a doily. I adjust my radio belt before I sit. From another chair, he lifts a small dozing dog, some blend of the popular miniature breeds filling our shelters. Consumed by maternal urges, a person will adopt a miniature as infant substitute. Enthusiasm is tested when the new owner discovers the dog has defecated in her handbag.

"My latest conquest." J.J. sets the dog on his lap, where it gnaws a patch of white lace along his zipper.

"How many would you say?"

"Conquests?" J.J. looks up, blinking.

"Dogs," I say.

"Oh." Silence. Then, "Who's counting?"

"For one, County," I say. "Though there is no canine numerical limit by dwelling—"

"There ought to be!"

"Well, J.J., there is a total number of registered complaints. This house is one complaint short of a forcible reduction."

"What are they saying?" He grins.

I refer to the file. "The following observation was made on Monday, June 15th, from an individual residing at the corner of 1666 NE 138th Street and Pleasant Street—"

"That's that fellow next door."

" 'It's packed with dogs in there,' " I read the complaint aloud. " 'I don't like dogs suffering. Some nights my wife cries herself to sleep just thinking on it.' "

"They should look in their own backyards," J.J. says. "The dears."

"To be fair, there's no denying the smell—"

"Not so bad once you're in?"

"Neighbors report never having seen a single canine out of doors."

"House trained, every last hound."

"And the waste?"

He commences to sing, high and flat, "All God's creatures got waste."

"May I make a friendly recommendation?" I say.

"Think I'll die in here and they'll eat me? You read about that."

"Do your own reductions, one *hound* a day. Take it to the shelter or give it to friends."

"Friends?" J.J. looks at me, longer than I'd deem necessary. He scoops up the dog on his lap. "Here."

"That's the idea."

"Here." He's pushing it at me. "Here."

Rule number six, avoid direct contact with animals.

"I cannot act as intermediary," I say. "You'll have to take it to the shelter."

"Such an intrepid woman as you must have offspring."

I reveal nothing. The personal is out.

"Have a heart." He sets the animal on my lap. I look down and see that it is not one of the miniature breeds. It's a puppy, the tender humid scent pushing up through the other smell.

"I can't," I say. "I'm not allowed."

"No?" he whispers into the puppy's ear. J.J.'s fastened silky hair cascades across my thighs.

"It's not County," I say. "It's my ex. He forbade me to bring more animals to our kid."

"Ow," he says, scooting his chair closer, "what did you bring to your child?" He pats my leg kindly. "Tell me everything."

"J.J., I brought her a kitten, the whole litter as matters go, a dog, pure bred, a conversant bird, a snake."

"A snake!" J.J. covers his eyes and winces.

Clarification is needed. "Pets are known to help children get over a split," I say. "But my ex complained about taking care of them."

"You poor creature!" J.J. says, "You just couldn't stop bringing them home." His shoulders quiver. His mouth spreads wide on big yellow teeth. He is laughing himself to bits.

Ha ha ha.

I give back the puppy.

I get to my feet, I say, "This is strictly a matter of animal control, which you are in direct violation under code 3883— sorry, no, that's not it."

"What is code 3883?" A meaty index finger paints the numbers in the air. "So shapely."

"3883 is code for ritual animal destruction."

"Oh, my." J.J. rises and adjusts his jeans then strides over to what must be a cupboard if the sound of tin cans knocking is indication.

"I've offended you, Ms. Stero."

"Negative." They think they can get to you.

J.J. squeezes down on a can opener. The tin clicks and gasps, salty and foul, and I am hit all over again with the living that smells in this house.

The dogs yip and claw and beat at their basement door.

"Cat food?" I say.

"Yeah, yeah, yeah." J.J. looks back at me and frowns. The can opener clatters to the counter. Sauntering over, J.J. reaches for my face, his salty fingertips hot, soft. "What's the matter, Ms. Stero?"

J.J.'s hip riding up at my radio is the matter. You can go heart to heart all you want, but in the end there's no knowing how an individual will behave under pressure.

"You."

"Dogs were the concern," J.J. says.

"You concern me—"

"The number in my home."

"People are their homes." I need to get some air. J.J.'s chin lifts. "Cute."

"Just something my kid said."

"Too bad about your kid."

"What?"

"I said too bad—"

"No, I meant what makes you say that, J.J., about my—"

"Easy now, Ms. Stero." J.J. drives his index finger between my teeth. Stunned, I am a bottle corked. My tongue shoves the finger out, but the finger pushes back. Probing its ridges, I grasp the digit between my cheeks. "Oh!" He yanks the finger out. "Don't suck it."

"*You* groped me!" I say, panting. "How dare you."

J.J. wipes his finger on his shirt. "I beg your pardon? The way you were breathing, worse than a snorting bull. Mother of God, I had to do something before you split in two, Ms. Stero."

I want to laugh. I am not without humor for how things can go. And all at once I do go, thin-skinned spasms, swoon—

"Oh no, Ms. Stero," J.J. says, catching me under the arm. "None of that."

He drags me into a room without windows that may have served as large pantry if the number of shelves is indication. The springs of the sofa twang beneath me as I turn my back to him and glare at dog fur sprouting from the brown velour cushion. J.J. returns a moment later, patting a feather duster along the heads of porcelain dogs sitting up on the shelves above. His apron swells into view. Above the ruffle runs a pattern of children netting butterflies. J.J. is whistling Snow White's song for cleansing the cottages of dwarves. She always sang that song, my little girl, Virginia.

At the sound of my gasp, he looks over. "You all right now, Ms. Stero?" He extends his hand to help me up. "It ain't exactly a fainting couch."

"It's not policy to faint." I get up on my own and walk, not run, to the front door.

"Oh, don't get all huffy," he says, following me into the hallway. "If it's about me putting a finger in your mouth? I can clear that up. Something sure set you off. All at once I've got a lady who is not breathing. You were turning blue, Ms. Stero. Blue. So I inserted my finger. I read it on a dog blog, 'Seven Surefire Remedies for Hyperventilation.'"

At the sound of their master's voice, a welter of noise starts up behind the basement door. I picture the whole mob packed in on the top two steps.

"Now, now," J.J. tells his dogs, "keep your coats on."

Their proximity reminds me that there is safety in duty. "I am here to inspect dogs. I haven't seen any. I am required to make a count. Open the door," I say. "That's an order."

J.J.'s eyes slide to the basement door then back to me. "Suspicion makes those baby blues appear small, Ms. Stero. Shame on you, your best feature." He steps toward me.

"No!" I step back. "Stay, you. Stay away."

His hands fly up. "Okay. Okay! Show yourself out!"

I'm back on the lawn, my heart pounding. The sun pitches behind the eave on his house, and I am cast in darkness. Across the street a child in the preschool wails, "Wah, wah, wah."

⸻

One) Debriefing.

"Canines," I say. "An excessive number inhabit the dwelling." Headquarters is dead except for the drone of barking dogs in sanitation.

"You get a count?"

"Negative."

Pedro's eyes fix on me. "You been lying down? Your hair. It's got that bed look."

"Pedro," I say, "the fact is that in spite of following procedure, I did not see any dogs." I carry the forms to my desk located directly across from Pedro's. The dogs in sanitation have quieted. I check the office clock. Feeding time. Pedro is still staring at me.

"So what they complaints about?" he says.

"The house does smell. There are canines in residence. I heard them." I look at my hands. "I held a puppy."

"Against policy, Stero."

Two) Bathroom break.

I walk out of the office and head down the corridor to the ladies and open a stall door and sit on the can. I think about unbuckling my belt and removing the pants in case I need to evacuate, but that all of a sudden seems like a lot of trouble.

The door opens and someone tiptoes in. I try to keep the noise down to a sniffle.

Pedro says, "Is that you crying, Stero?" His boots are visible in the stall beside mine. "For the last four year everybody round here been saying that Stero going to lose it one day. I tell them, nah man, Stero got guts behind those impressive set of . . . like that, you know. Look how fast she get back to work after that shit happen. Stero, she writing citations for excesses two to one over the other chingasos here." He clears his throat. "You took the loss like a man, Stero. What's hot is that you are a woman."

He rubs a sheet of toilet paper back and forth across the toe of his black boot until the paper breaks up and balls away. He stands and shuffles out the stall.

Three) I know what I have to do.

Pedro is at the coffee station pouring some in his mug. "I appreciate your loyalty, Pedro," I say, "but in point of fact I did seek treatment. The county therapist treated me for the mandated session. Her treatment consisted of a list of recommendations. One was to relinquish everything that reminded me of Virginia. I ever tell you how my ex dumped all her pets back on me?"

"You told me." He springs back to his desk.

I trail after Pedro and hand him the mug he left behind. "Pedro, what evidence do police require to get a DNA sample? Hair, nails, what?"

"That puppy was stolen?" Pedro whispers.

"Negative."

"You mean like hair from a people?"

"J.J. said, 'Too bad about your kid.' Pedro, why would J.J. say that?"

"J.J.?" Pedro frowns. "That a man or a lady?"

"Good question. We've got about a million ways to declare our sex and species. Why not make it plain and get on with living?"

"Stero, why you talking about this J.J.?"

"J.J. is the occupant of the house on Pleasant Street that's across from the Chrysalis Preschool."

"You said the house wasn't near no preschool."

———

J.J. lets his dogs out of the basement at night, a strategy to alert him to intruders no doubt. However not a single dog sounds the alarm when I climb in through the window, which of course is not standard procedure. Their tongues greet me, long stretches of saliva catching my fingers. The floorboards bend under the weight of them. I see now that what I took for wood siding in the hallway is in fact the swipe after swipe of unwashed dog. Although I managed to enter without recourse to a flashlight, the dogs are difficult to tell apart. Waiting until dawn failed to bring more light into this home. Nevertheless, I commence the count. "I cannot recommend it," the county therapist's warning suddenly rises up. "Further contact with animal hoarders puts you at risk."

The dogs climb over each other now, the smallest leaping from shoulder to shoulder and me, amid the shifting shapes, the panting, me, in the middle, this bitch one in the middle.

I shoo and kick to drive them off. Dog after dog funnels into the kitchen. Alone in the hallway now, I edge toward the basement door. Preparing myself for the door coming open, for the descent of the stairs, for the . . . *skritch-skritch*. What? My stomach tightens. Something—no *someone*—is scratching on the other side of the door. What sounded like one lone scratch is in fact soft flesh tapping and sliding down the wood. Smoothly, the knob turns in my hand. A little push and I'm in. Except that I'm not. The door's locked. Why locked when all the dogs are out? Why keep in a dog? Unless, of course, it's not a dog. I drop to the floor and prepare a few words to say through the slender crack beneath the door when a long hair wraps around my tongue. I hook it off with my nail. The strand is fine as the hair on the head of a child. A sob rises in me.

My radio goes off. "Stero, where you at? Come in. Will you come in, *mujer!*"

"Pedro," I whisper into my radio.

The overhead goes on. I get to my hands and knees. The dogs scramble out the kitchen, jamming up the hallway. At the other end stands J.J. in a nubby robe, hand on the light switch, squinting. "Ms. Stero?"

The scratching starts again on the other side of the basement door. "J.J.," I say, rising, radio slipping out my hand. "On behalf of East Valley Animal Control, I demand you open that door."

He frowns. "Ah, why?"

"I have reason to believe you hide someone." I dangle the long human hair between my finger and thumb. It catches the light like spun gold. "Is it a child? It's policy to ask."

J.J.'s brow has formed a deep and guilty V. "How did you

get in here?" He notices the window ajar and says, "Is that legal? I mean, don't you need a warrant or something?"

"A child is missing." I clasp the hair to my chest. "A little girl. Virginia was at the preschool when someone took her." A couple of dogs tilt their heads at me.

J.J. comes on so fast the dogs separate before him in that way you picture from the Bible. As he passes me, he takes my hand. His eyes flash. The dogs close back in, getting underfoot as he leads me down the hallway. "Ms. Stero, I have been patient. I made polite talk. But, come on, you're breaking the law." He lifts the latch on the front door. "Time to go."

"Not alone." I yank my hand out of his and wade back through the dogs to the basement door. But J.J. catches me by the shoulder. I knock him off with a good shove. Arms pinwheeling he topples back, grabbing the doorknob to brace his fall, which inadvertently throws the front door wide open. Dogs blast out the door, daft canine propulsion into the pale morning light. They scatter like jacks across the yard. A pit bull eases onto its haunches and drops a pile big as a melon onto the neighbor's lawn.

J.J. clambers to his feet. I turn to see him brushing aside strands of his blond hair sprung from the fastener. He inserts a key into the lock. "You missed one," he says, red faced. He pulls open the basement door. I hesitate and squint back out his front door. Across the street the teacher skips out of the Chrysalis Preschool, cheering on the loosed dogs. All this fresh air hovering on the threshold, and I can't get a decent breath.

The spill of morning light terminates at J.J.'s slippers, where the basement door now looms open. I march through the door but halt at the top step on account of the stench. Shadows cast by a bulb swaying on a cord contour the dirt floor below. I go down. Planked pine pops and snaps with each step into this space dug out from the earth, more cooling room than basement. Sweat trickles beneath my bra. Dragging my hand along the damp wall that seems to hum, my fingers launch indolent flies. Smell has taken on a kind of pneumatic shape, scorching the hairs in my nostrils. I reach the bottom step. Lining every wall are aquamarine garbage bags, three bags deep, knotted in neat bows. I taste supper at the back of my throat. Brow sweat cascades my palsied hands as I loosen the knot on one of the bags. A suck of breath. The bag blooms open. Lumped, coiled, and crumbled dog feces white-laced with mold fill the bag. I scan the other bags and recognize the outlines of dog waste in each.

What a smell. I gaze back down into the open bag and inhale.

Exhale.

Inhale.

J.J. is right. Not so bad. Even smells a bit fruity, marvelous as turned soil.

"Knock yourself out."

I had not heard J.J. come down and quickly try to close the bag.

"Don't be shy, Ms. Stero," he says. "We're all God's creatures."

His arms spread to encompass a long line of ceramic water bowls and a carpet of dog beds ordered and numbered. "Fifteen bowls, thirty-eight beds, sixty-six bags of poop." His eyes shift. "But who's counting?"

I follow his gaze to a kennel nestled in the middle of the dog beds, the puppy panting inside.

"Poor baby," I say, dropping to my knees before the kennel and reaching through the open door. "Where's Mommy?"

The puppy licks my knuckle, and I wiggle the tip of my finger into its mouth. "Ouch!" I say, looking up at J.J. "He bites!"

IN OUR HOUSE

NOBODY LIKES MY SISTER. EVEN SO, NOBODY'S KILLED her yet and she turns eleven today, so I'm baking her a birthday cake. It wasn't my idea. "God, take my right hand," Mother likes to say (though she doesn't believe in God), "I don't need it with Desiree to get the job done." She and Dad have gone to a farm for my sister's present.

This cake is a nightmare. Why Mother couldn't just pick something from a regular cake and frosting box, I don't know. There's a half dozen layers, and she bought unsweetened coconut—so I have to sugar it up with other ingredients. Will someone tell me why I'm going to this trouble when my sister hates coconut? She says it tastes like plastic feathers.

Maybe Mother doesn't really want my sister to eat it. "Jane

may be thin now," Mother says, "but it could catch up with her on the next mouthful." When it comes to Jane, Mother can't think straight. It doesn't stop with this recipe straight out of *Greatest Gourmet Challenges.*

Jane trudges in from outside.

Her shoe slaps the floor, and she's breathing like a hound after a race. That's because her sinuses are always congested. With all those allergies, you'd think she'd stay away from spring flowers. But the great outdoors are Jane's thing, so Mother stocks up on pocket-sized Kleenex packs to keep the cuffs of Jane's shirts clean. Just another of Mother's futile exercises—think Jane uses them?

"What's stinks?" Jane says, routing mud from the tread of her elevator shoe with a twig.

I point to the mess she's making.

She just glares at me then points to the mess I'm making on the counter.

"I'm baking your birthday cake," I say.

"How come Mom's not making it?" She's rifling through Dad's tool drawer now.

"Mom's getting your present." The rabbit is a surprise.

"She better get me that fucking rabbit," she says, waving a pair of wire cutters for the hutch she's building, and limps out the back door again.

My sister has a terrible mouth. None of us can quite remember when it started. Dad likes to say, "Perhaps it was the baby bottle that elicited the first curse." To which I say, "Good thing Mother breast-fed me." Washing Jane's mouth out with soap or dabbing hot sauce on her tongue only spices up the curses, so now Mother and Dad ignore. The other day I told Jane she sounded like her dad was a drunken sailor, and Mother slapped my face—the first time in my twelve years. "You should know better than that, Desiree." Sailors are a sensitive topic in our house. Both Jane's dad and mine are in the Navy. Dad's a Lieutenant, though.

"Perfect, Desiree," Mother says as I pull the cake pans out of the oven, the third and final stage of the leavening process.

"Damn ridiculous cake," I say.

"You sound like your sister," says Dad, setting a cardboard box on the floor.

"Desiree will never talk like her sister," Mother says, thumbing off her high heels. "She doesn't have the vocabulary." She hands me the china cake plate with the marine blue trim. It's printed in gold with my name and date of birth (we don't have a plate with Jane's name).

"Oh," I say, "I know the words, Mother. The skill comes in not using them."

Dad winks at me, believing I am witty. He lifts off the lid of the cardboard box.

Long, long ears rise up.

"Is it the one she wanted?" I say, watching the nose flick along the rim of the box.

"It's a rabbit," Dad says.

"Good enough," Mother says.

I wonder if it is. If anything is.

Jane has opened her presents and is reading out loud from the book I gave her called *Amazing Animals Facts*. The rabbit sits in the cardboard box on the dinner table. She's named him Rude Boy.

"Listen to this, Desiree," Jane says as she jams her toe into the heel of her elevator shoe. She does this, I've noticed, when she's really excited. "The female pond snail's vagina is in her head."

Mother hands me the cake knife from the good-silver drawer after I light eleven blue candles. Through the little flames I see Jane's face above the book, the pale, veined skin set against the black, black hair, not a bit like Mother's. But it's a pretty face, if only she'd smile.

"The female octopus has got its vagina in her nose." Jane reads aloud, "If approached by the male octopus when not in season, the female octopus will bite off his penis—"

"That's enough, Jane." Dad snatches the book out of her hands.

"A female tortoise gets itself ready to mate," Jane goes on from memory now, "by eating its own—"

"Cake," I say, as I set it on the table, beside the box. The candlelight edging the rabbit's ears in red.

"Happy Birthday to you," Dad sings in an operatic voice that makes us laugh.

I whisper, "Make a wish, Jane."

Pushing right up close to the cake, my sister laps up frosting with her tongue. "Coconut," she says. "Fucking-A!"

"Blow out the candles, Janey," Mother says, sounding ready for bed.

Jane blows and the room goes dark.

"Mama, I want to cut the cake," Jane says, reaching for the knife in my hand.

I look at Mother.

"The cake's very delicate, Jane," Mother says, turning the cake plate toward me. "Your sister will cut it."

"Bullshit! It's my birthday cake," Jane says, prying my fingers off the knife handle. The cake teeters—so many layers—as the knife drops from my hand and strikes the table. The rabbit leaps out of the box, spooked, hind legs knocking the cake platter. Cake and plate balance at the table's edge. Then crash. The plate hits the floor and explodes. Porcelain splinters. A sliver shoots like an arrow into the thick part of Mother's heel. She stares at the thing, maybe waiting for blood, but this, this is a clean puncture.

A hind leg thumps the rug, thumps the rug.

"Get rid of that damned animal," Mother says.

Dad hits Jane harder than I've ever seen him hit anything. Jane stumbles out of her shoe to fall on the floor.

"Help your mother," Dad tells me, as he picks up the rabbit by the neck's loose skin. He reaches out a hand to Jane. "Come outside, Jane," my father says. She takes his hand, solemnly, mute for a change, and they go outdoors, Jane without her shoe.

"It's her birthday!" Mother calls sadly after them.

Mother falls in love with sailors, but doesn't like the sea. Only once did she swim in it. "The current pulled me out where I didn't want to go," she says. After Mother married Dad, she cooked us three squares a day in their navy-issued kitchen. Until one morning when she stirred up the oatmeal then left it beside me in my highchair. She walked out of the house and hopped into the car of a sailor driving to his base on the West Coast. Eight months later she called Dad. Scarlet Fever must have sounded pretty bad. The very next day she was spooning soup into my mouth over the big ball of her stomach. When

Jane's time came, my mother refused to abandon her sick child, even as they handed her into the ambulance. It's to Jane's credit she made it out of Mother's belly at all. One leg shorter than the other was a small price to pay for a mother who hollered in the delivery room, "It got in there without my consent, it can get out by its own self."

Jane likes to say that the sailor in California might have made a swimmer of Mother if she'd stayed. Jane can say whatever she likes. Mother came back to Dad and me.

"Desiree," Mother says, and it occurs to me that my name suits me well. She hands me a trash bag.

The cake slumps upside down but intact on the floor. Mother kisses me on the crown of my head before turning to the stairs, taking one step at a time, fingers looped through the straps of her high heels. Mother is babying her injured foot.

Dad swings open the back door. The twilight in glorious ink behind him before the door bangs shut. His cheeks are red and his large hands hang at his sides. He doesn't see me as he follows Mother up the stairs. I scoop cake into the trash bag.

I'm sorting through the broken pieces of plate, determined to find the bit with my name on it, when I see Jane's shoe, every scary rubbery black inch of it. Outside she's sitting with her dead rabbit stretched across her legs. Her sock maybe bunched at the heel. I don't think she's angry. She knows how it is in our house.

I push my toes inside Jane's elevator shoe. The stiff leather cuts into my ankle as I get my balance. Though I'm older, we wear some of the same clothes, Jane and I. Still I am surprised by the fit. I wonder if Jane has tried on some of my shoes, pretending she's me. I walk in a circle, going up, then slamming down on the other foot. How does Jane do it, come and go as she does? On me, the shoe is ugly, but not on Jane. On her, on Jane, the ugly shoe fits.

Jane taps on the kitchen window above the sink.

I hobble over in her shoe.

When I open the window, she's yawning. "Are Mom and Dad in bed?"

"Probably asleep," I say. "Sorry about your bunny," I say.

"What?"

"I'll say a prayer," I say.

"Say what you want," Jane says. "He's sitting in the hutch. Dad said keep him outdoors until Mom cools off."

"Oh," I say, "I knew that."

"Seen my shoe?" she says. "My foot's cold."

"No."

"Take off the fucking shoe, Desiree."

"Say it nicely," I say. "You know, Jane, people will like you more if you do."

MIS-SAYINGS

CHIP SAYS, "BALLET IS HOW YOU SAY IT. Say it," he says.

"Belly," I say.

He says, "That's your stomach."

"Belly?" I say.

"Ballet," he says.

How I say what I say in his language I will get right some time. There are no words with rrr to stutter my tongue like in Russian. They called it a defect, that I could not get the rrr to roll out my tongue—I and others like me. Leave Russia to come up with a sound many Jews cannot make.

Dancer is what I wrote in the classified ad. Did I say what kind of dancer? It wouldn't matter—Chip says, "Ballet is how you dance there."

That I dance caught his taste for thumb-tip nipples, no
boob, all the fat a toe dancer can spare. "I can get to that live
thing inside a woman," Chip says, "when her boobs are small."

The big size of my boobs, you notice them first, before my
face. In my picture, they were there. I am the third girl Chip
has sent for after meeting through a picture. Of the girls
before, Chip says, "You can't get it right from a picture."

Possible getting it right is not all we are after.

The classified ad Chip wrote said conveyer, import/export,
foreign goods. I am his import. But it's the Russia in me—this
is what is foreign.

Chip takes out Chinese when I line my cook pots on his
stove. Not a pot in the kitchen when I arrived, mine under my
arm, many pots of many shapes in a box that had pressed into
my side since I took the plane out of Russia. I brought these
pots believing that enough pots in a kitchen can make a home,
but Chip has never tasted my cooking.

The doorbell rings, and Chip goes fast to the door, faster
than I can. "Hey, hey, man," he says, opening the door only
enough to get only himself out to the corridor.

When Chip comes back in, he is counting money but he
has no cartons of food. The first few times I asked where was
the take-out Chinese.

"I'll show you," Chip said.

Show is how Chip tells. We met, really, at the airport where
he showed himself by pointing to himself, said "Chip, Chip,"
then he took my hand in his very big hand and made a fist to
say we are together now. Straight to the grocery aisles after
that. Tap-tap on the butcher's glass, Chip nodding his head of
long hair at the layers of local meat, nodding until I did, too.

Bananas he balanced on his palm while the other hand ran over rounder fruits. Did I see what all there was?

His apartment, my new home, got a quick show. I stayed on in the bathroom—for the size of it—even after he shut off the light. The size of rooms swells in dark mirrors. Chip had more to show: a show was on TV of two men at a woman, the man on the rear, spanking her. I sat down and watched skin on the woman's thigh ripple with each slap, and I was happy.

Chip thought to show me all the things I could now have in America, but of all the things I had gone without, sex was not one of them. I laughed at this, making Chip smile. Then I got the shirt over my head and saw his face fall at the size of them. I took his head to them, anyway. His hand came up and covered my mouth. He said, "You okay?" Under Chip's hand I was still laughing, thinking of all he could show me.

"It's Chip," he said, "not cheap."

"I know," I said, but what I wanted to say was two languages stumble through my head, both fools.

Chip worked on how I said things. "TV is a tool," he said. We watched, Chinese cartons tossed in the bed. In such remains we did sex. "Man, you learned to fuck in the old, old country," Chip said.

"What of the girls before me?" I said.

"I want arms," he said, "arms that hold."

"Didn't the girls' arms hold?" I said.

"They weren't long enough," Chip said, opening my arm up, "they weren't ballet dancer's arms."

Hours, days in Chip's hold carry me to black waters that rise beneath my feet, shoelessly hanging off railings. Mother lays a cloth by the sea, and we eat hardboiled eggs with salt until the waters build up and blacken. Then I run, her hand up my arm, back to where it's safe on the railings. Where Mother promises black waters don't dare touch your soles. Watch the course of the baby's carriage cutting ridges in amounted snow; and in it my brother, so small. The carriage goes nicely on skis. One push too hard and down he'd go. Nooooo. This is milk Mother carries for her own mother; milk whitening a glass cupped against the pull and go of the street rail. Milk one day she will allow me to carry. Until then I watch to see if it spills on Mother's skirt. They watch, too— the other men riders. Mother is so pretty, and this is why they watch; but she says they watch the gypsies like that, too.

Carried, I am carried over to these rememberings by Chip, my conveyer.

I laugh, nervous again of this place—Chip's place—where all is new, his country so new even the trees are older than anyone's memory of them. And nervous of this language, too, where there is no rrr to stutter my tongue; and if there were, would anyone listen for it?

What Chip needed and what I needed, we got in bed. We did not get out, unless doorbells called.

I have waited for a time when Chip goes away for longer than the short time he takes out in the corridor, longer than it takes to take out Chinese. The things to pack can't be hurried. I had fewer things in Russia than now, and it took me years to get out.

It is true I could stay in Chip's hold and only see what he wants to show. What he doesn't want to show he keeps behind the door, in the corridor. It would not be so hard not to see. It is not so hard for Chip. When he hears I danced, he sees only the ballet, a handkerchief-lace body propped up and spun again and again. But it is because I danced that I see past closed doors into corridors. It is because I danced that I smell past closed doors into corridors where Chip stands in corners with this or that guy who stinks like he will come open if he doesn't get some of what Chip sells in his vein, in his nose, in his gut. It is because I danced a kind of dance I can never show to Chip that I do know. I know that I did not come this long way from a Russia, where business is done mostly in dark, to an America where dark business has just moved out to the corridor.

Start with my pots. They stack back into their box, and I think, maybe if I had cooked for Chip. I think maybe I must think about me, about how I will need money. A city like this, some streets cost just to walk down. I think now I am not so different than the girls before me—so what if he says I have arms that hold—I'm just another that Chip imported but did not marry. So maybe I will have to do my dance again.

The doorbell rings. My suitcase is filled but still open.

Ring-ring.

"Wait," I call, guessing that on the other side of the door is just one who buys from Chip in the corridor.

I open the door, wider than Chip does. Why hide dark business in the corridor anymore—it was me Chip was hiding it from. A man is there, a boy-man who has braided his beard and likes eating too much. He sees them first, my boobs of course, then my face.

"Chip's not here," I say.

He says, "That true?"

"Do you see him?" I let him look right in.

He doesn't look. He comes in close to me and pulls a scissors out of his pants. Such scissors children use to carve pictures. He tilts them up at me. I step back into the apartment. "Come in," I say. "But put those away."

He follows me into the apartment that does have souvenirs from other countries, like the X of the Southern flag Chip says is good for covering cracks left by earthquakes.

I see that the scissors are put away before I tell the—call him a boy—to please sit down. I start loading my last bag, with shoes.

He sits on the couch, placing jumpy hands first on his knees then on the table. "Going on a trip?" he asks.

I say, "I am coming from one."

He says, "I hate coming home."

"It is only home if that is what you left," I say. Zip up the bag, snap close the suitcase.

"You're packing," he says. "Chip doesn't know, does he."

"What does Chip know?" I say.

He laughs, looks around. His leg is jumping now so he slaps a thigh. "It's Chip," he says. "Maybe it's better how you say it."

I laugh. "Thank you."

"Where's the can?" he says.

I look around, think, what can?

This he has no patience for. Through the bedroom to the bathroom he goes on legs jigging loose in loose trousers. Drawers and cupboards bang shut over the sound of things spilling and pinging against the sink.

Pills tumble from the boy's jittery hands as he scoots out

the bathroom. They drop into the rug when he eases onto the couch. Down I go on my knees, picking out red and yellow from between threads, dropping the pills back into his palms. His eyes are on them again. I look down and understand. From where he sits, my boobs are something.

"They for real?" he asks.

"What is 'for real,'" I say.

His face asks is she simple? "They a part of you," he says, "or the doctor rig them up?"

"Chip says, 'No matter how warm it gets, women's nipples stay cool,'" I say. "Maybe only the nipples are for real." How Chip says things doesn't always sound right but this is what I like. From the first time we held each other, he said our bodies fit together like bark fits to tree.

"Who is the tree," I said, "and who is the bark?"

"You are my tree," he said, "my tender, tender tree."

The boy comes from the kitchen with a bottle of juice. He points at my suitcase. "What're you waiting for?" he says. "Hoping Chip'll show up and stop you?"

I smile. This boy may know some things. "I need a plan," I say.

He lays the pills out on the table, grouped by colors and size, this army. "Start with a map," he says.

Whose map? Chip said not to lose him in the immigration building and when I lost him, I studied a map on a wall, arrows pointing up and down floors to arrows pointing to exits. A map is not the same from language to language. Pushing up on me to read the map were more people from my country, also confused with maps, shouting to each other in their language that makes my hands sweat. The map told me where I was, but I knew where I was—I was lost without Chip.

The boy puts Chip's medicines onto his tongue, one pill at a time, following with a swallow of juice. The hand holding the bottle shakes so he can't get his lips tight on the rim. Fluid works into the weave of his beard. He sets down the bottle.

"What's the accent?" he says.

"I am from Russia," I say.

"Like those guys in the park who cheat at dominoes?"

"Do they speak with accent?"

"Who doesn't speak English with an accent," he says, this American says.

I say, "It's how Jews speak Russian that makes us alike."

"How do you speak Russian?" he says.

"With an accent," I say. "Do you see?"

He shrugs and goes back to the pills. Sealed beneath foil is a flu cure. These tablets are not easily available. He pulls out his scissors to cut the foil, but no such luck. Shit scissors.

He looks back at me. "You speak English with an accent. You speak Russian with an accent." He says, "Where don't you speak with an accent?"

I knock on my skull.

"Words," he says.

That was good. We have become familiar. I have less and less to hide. He is willing to see. The boy sets aside the flu cure. Enough is enough. He sits back, looks at his hands.

"Where'd he go?" he says.

"To buy tickets," I say. "A Russian ballet is in town."

"Chip buys tickets to ballets?"

"He hoped I would get him in free," I say. "I dance," I say.

"You're no ballerina," he says.

"Well, I know a dance," I say. I lift my box and pick up my

suitcase and bag.

"Let me help you," the boy says, grabbing my suitcase.

"No, thank you."

I step around him, going toward the door. From behind, he puts his hands on my hands. One of his hands holds the scissors. I try to pull away, but he's not letting go, and the scissors gathers my skin between its blades.

"Thank you," I say and let go. The box I was holding drops to the floor and a lid to a pot shoots out.

"Do you know what kind of dancer I am?" I say.

"I can guess," he says.

"I'll show you," I say. "I'll show you now."

The boy takes the suitcase and bag off me and carries them to the couch and sits down next to them. He puts the scissors on the table and waits for what I will do next.

What I do is better done with music, layers of air, some crowd. This boy, he doesn't even smoke. Maybe the pills washing into his blood will create atmosphere.

Take a time, go inside. There, in my skull. Start the movement on the outside.

The body remembers. My hands push down on my stomach, fabric spreading fingers wide. Between the hips my hands go. Hot, hot, to the seat of myself. One foot on the table, skirt slips away to thigh. Arch back, the shirt flaps, opening to skin. Take away the bra, the thing that hates to let boobs go. Fucking hooks. Can't get them . . .

My audience is up, on his feet.

This show must go on!

Yes, yes! No hiding now.

His scissors cold mouth my skin, gumming at the bra strap.

I laugh and allow the pill-swallower to dig and twist my boobs free from Russian machining.

The bra is cut. Shake, and the straps knock down around my arms, and the bra swings from my wrist to the floor. Dance now and sing the song, the one that turns young cheeks red. Sing:

I was a little dressmaker.
I stitched a wavy pattern.
But now I am an actress
And I've become a slattern.

I look at the boy a little to see if he likes my song and to see how my dance works on him.

He looks back at me—but kindly.

Could be the pills have taken measure of what is sad and sick in a life and dissolved a dose into his soul. He picks up my shirt and brings it around me in a warm and wrapping motion. I can stop the dance now but I don't want to. The truth was not so hard to show, after all, and I can dance and dance for it. Secretive smiling like a drunk, the boy seems to know this, too. Finally, I sit beside him to find my breath, but he has already gone sleepy with pills. I look at this boy, thankful for his audience, but wishing it was Chip I did the dance for.

Chip said import/export. He didn't say what of. He didn't have to. Behind doors, exchanges in corridors, soon Russia is not so foreign. Only with Chip it's worse—with him, I must pronounce ballet.

It's not what you say, but how. Was it how I said what I said that gave him the idea?

Dancer.

Conveyer.

Words, they float to the surface, coating with alikeness. Finding the exception in one from the next, this is the place where what we say can make room for what we really are.

Say, I am a Russian. What kind?

With an accent. What kind?

Sure, a Russian accent when I talk to America, but how is it called an accent in Russia, where I never spoke in any other tongue? Is it how I say it or how it sounds, this accent, this scent of outsider that leaves its scent on every language that I speak? Every language except what would be my own— Mother's tongue, blood tongue—a language that I have never known, and so can never speak.

Could I make for Chip a place to say what he really is? Say, a man. What kind of man? Good, bad, new, old—newly bad, maybe, but never old enough. Hearing accents is an art very much older than the first memory an American has of trees.

What kind of boobs? Large boobs.

Chip likes them small.

Still they are boobs. The nipples are cool, no matter the size, cool against his naked chest that fits so well to mine when I am in his hold. When I am in his hold, the waters rise and the blades of the baby carriage cut and the milk whitens—in his hold, my first memories speak without accent.

I should leave my pots. Chip must learn cooking, to stop taking out.

Possible I will stay a little longer to cook him a meal— something hot and teasing on the tongue. Chip could have a taste for it, after all.

TO SKIN A RABBIT

THE RABBIT IS FRESHLY KILLED. I PLACE IT back down on the board
and start directly in the middle of the stomach, cutting
until I reach the throat. I'm careful not to pierce the membrane. When blood appears, I blot it with cornmeal.

Father says, "A science log keeps everything in order." This is
my first science log. This is also the first time I've skinned a
warm-blooded animal. Father doesn't know I have the rabbit.
I had to break its neck.

To proceed one must have the following materials: 1) needle
and thread, 2) cornmeal, 3) cotton batting, 4) one-sided razor,

5) forceps, 6) scissors, 7) 2 feet of 1/6" wire, 8) pliers, 9) arsenic. Father won't buy me arsenic. He says no girl needs arsenic before the age or 12.

From the central opening, I cut 2/3 the way down through the skin to the middle of each hind leg. With the razor, I cut the skin around the anus to that I can force the skin back with my fingers until my thumb and forefinger meet the other hand around the animal's spine.

Then "tug the skin off," as Father says, "like you would a tight coat."

I have skinned and dissected snakes (without the arsenic, their skins attract insects). Skinning rabbits isn't much different. However, this one is different. As an example of its species, it's unremarkable, but I am skinning the rabbit to officially mark this day. I won't be taken in again.

It will take my father longer. "I am building up resistance to your mother," Father tells me, "the way the hull of a boat collects barnacles."

From the taut muscle membrane along the hind legs, I've worked the skin free with the razor. No wonder rabbits can hop straight in the air like they do. With my scissors, I cut about midway between the joints through each thighbone. After slicing the meat from each bone, I leave the cleaned lower bones attached to the skin.

More cornmeal to blot the blood. I can use as much cornmeal as I like, Father says.

My father, the marine biologist. He lets me work the whale watching cruise boat he captains. It's rained for the past two weeks, and we haven't seen a humpback in the channels for almost as long.

Mother came on board yesterday with the 31 other passengers. At first I didn't recognize her. She'd tucked her hair up into a hat that mostly hid her face. She wore square-shaped black sunglasses and a raincoat that fit her like a glove. "I'm incognito," she said and handed me a hatbox with small holes punched in the top. It was tied with a ribbon. "Happy Easter," she said. She smelled like gin. I put the box aside, near the captive pelican on the rear deck. My mother is not allowed to see me. "You shouldn't be here," I told her. "He'll be mad.

I'm allowed to include this in my science log. It's proof of Father's warning: "Don't keep unstable chemicals close to your physical person." If Mother were a fairy, she'd throw dust in your eyes.

With my fingers, I push the skin off the spine and away from the tail. When the muscles cling, I use the razor. I am careful not to cut the skin around the tail.

"There goes Peter Cotton Tail, hopping down the bunny trail," Mother said when the boat started rocking. "Don't tell your father I'm on board," she said. "It'll be our little secret." She always makes me lie to him.

I pull the bony tail right out of its skin. All the way down each foreleg I slit the muscle with scissors, same routine as the thighs.

Mother reached for the handrail to steady her. "What's that?" she said as I crouched down to look in the pet carrier. "This," I told her, "is a juvenile male pelican. He injured himself previously and was nursed at the research center." The joints in my mother's knees cracked as she knelt down beside me. Tucking my hair behind my ear she said, "You sound more like your father every day. Why can't you just talk like a kid?"

Now, pushing away from the abdomen with my fingers, I loosen all the skin up to the head (it was easier with the snake, the head and tail being all of a piece). I keep pushing the skin so it goes over the head. When it sticks, I use the razor. One must take care with the ears. They're easy to feel, not easy to see. The rabbit is a juvenile. A bunny, as Mother would say.

Dall porpoise swam besides the boat. I pointed out to Mother the large white area along the vent region that distinguishes the mammal. 8 knots, the speed of the Captain's boat, wasn't much fun for these fast swimmers. My father made a similar comment over the loud speaker in the con. Mother was lucky he couldn't see her from there.

Mother complained that I wouldn't be going to church tomorrow. "I'll pray for you and your father," she said. I turned to look at her, but I only saw myself and the bow of the boat in her glasses. "Hungry, darling?" Mother said.

The eyes are black lumps. The film that covers them extends far back on the head. It's important to cut through the length of the film. Last to come off are the lips. In cutting through the fleshy part of the lips, upper and lower, the skin finally detaches from the body. I thread my needle and sew the two lips together, knotting off their tips.

"Collections are best if they tell a story," Father says. When I've completed the job, I'll have a study skin for my collection. I'll fill out the card detailing the specifics of the specimen and tie it around the leg. The card will supply the answers to what, where, when, and length. But nobody will read how that skin makes me feel.

Mother backed against the cabin wall and slid down onto the bench seat. "Are you all right, Mother? Should I get you something?" She pressed her fingers to her closed lips and swallowed something back then hid her fingers in the folds of her coat. When she looked up, her eyes wove with ideas. "Do you think I should eat? I haven't today." I ordered a burger for her. Unlike Father and me, she'll eat meat.

The cook was in the cabin grilling when Mother ran past him to the toilet. The sound of her vomiting was audible over the spitting grease. "Samantha, you better get up on deck," the cook said as he set another patty on a bun. "Your father's calling on the intercom." The cook borrows my ponytail holders for his long hair and he always knows where I should be. Mother wouldn't open the toilet door. I wondered how she kept up vomiting on an empty stomach.

Once the skin is free, it's advised to throw away the body but keep the head. I'd never throw away the body. You don't go on an Easter egg hunt, find a colored egg, and discard the stuff inside the shell. This skin is for my collection. Other questions are answered through study of meat and bones.

The boat's engine was idling. I knew where we were. Father always stopped at Gull Island to lecture about the birds. Standing beside him in the con was where he liked me now. I tapped softly again on the toilet door. The paper plate in my hand blotted the burger grease.

Time to coat the skin with arsenic, which I don't have. Father warns arsenic can get in your mouth when you bite your nails. I chew mine until they bleed. He says I'll quit the biting once I put my mind to it, but I could just wear gloves with the arsenic.

I cut the wire and form it into an oblong. After rolling a sheet of cotton batting around the wire, I shove the form down into the empty tail. Care must be taken, as the skin can rip. The same kind of wire and cotton configuration is used for the body, but larger. Same wire and cotton on the legs, but smaller.

I hotfooted it to the con. The captain looked at me in that way he does. I've teased him about it, calling him Snake Eyes. Then he looked down at the hamburger. "Where were you?" he said. Seagulls flew in a circle right over his head. Funny, it made me think of a halo. "I felt lightheaded," I lied. "Thought I'd eat something sustaining." The captain threw the engine into reverse. He started talking over the loud speaker about keeping an eye out for sea lions hiding in the rocky outcroppings on the next island.

With the forceps I knead the cotton batting into a hard tip. I'm supposed to push the tip of the cotton batting all the way to the rabbit's nose. "Nose to nose," as Father says.

A lot of passengers had lined up to use the toilet. I knocked on the door. "Please, Mommy, come out." The cook went up for the captain. I ran out to the small toilet window at deck level. Mother's foot in the sneaker with no laces was all I could see. I opened the window and started to squeeze through. My shirt pocket caught on the window frame, which tugged the shirt up around my head. The boat tilted and I fell in, landing on top of her. Could have broken her spine. I saw the captain's legs march by the window. Pulling her up by the shoulder from the damp floor, I helped Mother sit. "Do you suppose He got sea sick walking on all that water?" she said. The smell in there was ammoniac, the small window insufficient ventilation. I inched open the toilet door. Father stood on the other side, so I slammed it shut. Locked it. "Hippety-hoppity, Easter's on its way," Mother sang. "Talk about second chances. That's the resurrection of Christ in an eggshell." She winked at me. "Sometimes heaven's too good for it angels." Salt water dusted Mother's skin. As she wrapped her arms around me, I felt the drag of tiny grains against my skin. She closed her eyes. "When you were in my stomach," she said.

The captain pushed his weight against the locked door.

"Stand back everybody," I heard him say. "We have an emergency."

"You said it," a passenger joked. It must have been a joke.

The tips of Mother's fingers pushed at my cheek. "I remember feeling you shake in my belly, quaking under my skin." She smiled and one eye opened, red. "Gin, even then." Mother's scary because you don't know what you'll get with her. Father used to like that about her. "But then she was the only baby in the house."

If you peel the shell from a hard-boiled egg, bit by each sharp bit, then you'll have a smooth, perfect shape. That's how simple the truth is. "What's inside the Easter egg?" she said as the door flew open, right off its hinges. The captain had found us.

"This is entirely inappropriate," he said. As he carried Mother out of the toilet, her hand searched the air for mine.

She said, "You haven't opened my Easter present."

Father ordered me up on deck. I wasn't allowed below again. The boat surged forward. The captain was back at the helm. From the hatbox I heard a scrambling sound, like dry rice dropping on the floor. I pulled the ribbon and lifted the lid. Inside was the juvenile rabbit.

Through the port vent to the cabin I heard Father talking to the cook. "She'll always be my responsibility," he said, "so long as she keeps finding a way back in." He ought to be smarter than that.

Mother doesn't fool me anymore. I can see right through the skin, the meat, the bone, to the very core, which is just blood that you can blot up with cornmeal, if you have enough.

I take my needle and thread and stitch the skin together from the throat down to the tail. I make sure to pull tight together the two edges of the skin. Holding the specimen, I straighten out the legs and tail in a natural way. I am kneading the body with my fingers until its shape appears as it did in life.

That's how to skin a rabbit.

MY HUSBAND'S SON

HADN'T EXPECTED MY HUSBAND'S SON. HOW COULD I? I had no idea my husband had a son—another son. I suppose there was always the possibility. A foreign life such as my husband had led might include having other children while in the company of other women. But even so, even if my husband had brought about others, I didn't imagine one would pay us a visit.

My husband's son had not met his father. Not here and not over in their own country. My husband's country is the sort of place where that sort of thing could happen. That's why he left. I've never asked him if that was why. You assume those things in a marriage like mine.

My husband said, when he got off the phone, after he'd made another drink, that he wasn't surprised about his son's visit and it didn't bother him. I'm not like my husband. I don't like it when the phone rings and I'm not expecting a call. Our dogs have a bark that tells me a visitor's arrived. I don't like hearing that bark when I've invited no one. Now a surprise here and there, I don't object to that. Imagine my surprise the day our son, our own son, arrived. He wasn't due yet. My husband wasn't surprised. He was waiting for me at the hospital. He said he knew.

My husband's not some gypsy fortuner. He is a foreign man. How much can one ever know about that kind of man? He has a whole personage that doesn't include me. I don't object to this. It can be sexy imagining the partners he might've been with. Imagine, he partnered with them in a foreign tongue. I can't say it's sexy to think of him having partnered with other women now. Now that I know what this partnering produced. Nothing's sexy where children are concerned.

I chose sweets from the imported-food section of the store for the visit. I asked my husband how to pronounce the sweets' name when he called to say he'd be late.

"Just put them out prettily on a plate," he said. He asked what I had in mind for dinner for his son.

"I thought sweets," I said.

"He's not a child," my husband said.

This surprised me. Not that my husband's foreign son was no longer a child. Our own son had long ago stopped sucking on sweets and he was born after this other one.

"Why would I just buy sweets?" I said to my husband.

"That's how you want it," he said and we both laughed. My husband says such things because he sees the best in me. "I'll fix dinner," he said. He'd do that by having a pizza delivered to the house.

People often say how funny my husband is in our language. I confess that's certainly what caught my ear. Then they say to me, "Do you speak his?" They're always surprised when I say, "I have enough trouble with my own." But I'm not joking. I'd been hired to teach it to foreigners—and fired. "So that's how you met your husband," they will usually say next, "in the classroom?" I don't like to betray expectations. But the truth is my husband and I met in a bar.

It was at a time when I was uncomfortable with myself. I'd been feeling this way for longer than you'd expect from a woman who was just a couple years more than a girl. It made me ugly. What I mean is, though I'm a big girl and clumsy, I could have still been pretty, but I wasn't.

"Why feel comfortable?" my husband said. "You're not a stupid woman."

Being a foreigner can make my husband put things in strange ways in our language. The words lose a native speaker's sensitivity. Things get unruly. Never know who they will hit.

I don't have the first idea if my husband's funny in his own language. The fact is, I don't know very much about my husband's life in his country. Not beyond what he's told me, which is the little he wants to remember.

Marriage to a foreigner is a lonely place. There are whole locales where you feel dumb. His memories are in foreign words, and I've given up on translation. Where I stay now is here in this house in this language. That is my marriage.

So, funny was something I intended to look out for with his foreign son's visit. I'd see if he laughed at what his father said. Honest-to-goodness laughter takes you by surprise. Surprised is surprised, I don't care in what language. But not just funny. Visiting with his foreign son was quite a chance for my husband to talk. He might say words in combinations that would let something unexpected get out. "The more you talk," my husband says, "the more you give yourself away."

The dogs barked, and there at the door stood a young man with pizza. I thought that's him, my husband's son, he's delivering. Pizza is often delivered by men with accents.

This young man didn't have an accent that I could hear. That is to say, he didn't say anything. He just handed me the pizza.

"My husband ordered it," I said.

He nodded.

I said, "Your Dad."

He spoke up then. "Dad?" he said. "Dad?"

I knew then that I'd made a mistake. "Here's your money," I said. "Go on now."

I showed the dogs into the yard and hurried back to the couch. The TV played on but I was listening for the door. When the dogs barked from the yard, I was ready. I swung wide the front door. There he was. "You must be—"

He nodded. Such a nice smile, different.

"Please come in. My husband—he'll be here. Just late."

I escorted him into the living room. This cluttered living room of ours makes you ask for other rooms. The entire big room, and it is big for the size of our house, looks as though someone used it to recover from a long illness. "I'm afraid I don't speak a word," I said, "but we'll manage." I patted the cushion beside me for him to sit.

He didn't sit. He stared at me, clearly confused.

"Of your language!" I said. "I don't speak it."

He sat down on the couch now, so I offered sweets. He ate one, making a face that said tasty.

"I'd offer spirits," I said, "but we drink them up whenever we expect a visitor."

A funny sound came out of him.

"Oh, god," I said, "is it the sweets?" I patted his back. "You know," I said, "I hope you can't understand a thing I say."

He smiled just a touch then turned to the TV screen. I studied him. "You don't look like my husband. You take after your mother, I suppose." Casual was how I put this: "Has he stayed in touch with her, your mother I mean?"

The young man had no reply.

I said again, louder, "My husband, has he stayed in touch with her?"

He turned to me, but still nothing.

"Look at me asking you! I keep thinking you speak English. I'm very stubborn that way." He was beginning to make me mad. "My husband and I are very close, actually. He's told me a lot about his former life."

I got up to go. My husband's son grabbed my arm, drawing me back. I almost lost my footing. What a commotion. Now he was pointing at his tongue, saying, "Aaaaaah." Saying, "Aaaaguh."

All I could see was the sweet going to sugar on his tongue.

"What's wrong?" I said. "Can't you talk?"

I sat back down because I think I finally understood. "You can't. You poor dear, you can't talk!"

He shook his head, sorrily, inevitably, charmingly.

"Does your father know? I mean, of course, he knows?"

He looked down at the sweets. He took the time to choose another.

"You can't talk at all? Nothing, not a word?"

He lifted his hands, palms up, empty.

"Oh boy," I said.

Then I thought about it. What the hell is life for, anyway? Something new. At least this was something new.

But before I could ask how he lost the use of his voice, he stood up, brushed down his slacks, and marched out the living room.

I found him at the staircase where we'd framed pictures of our life, which was really our son. My husband's son didn't look like ours. Each son took after his mother, I suppose. With a tap at the corner of each photograph, he selected out pictures of our son in high school sports uniforms. We'd pinned up a lot of those.

"Our son liked the uniforms," I said. "Do you like sports?" I sounded like a mother.

He made out to be kicking a soccer ball, returning a tennis ball, shooting a basket. Then two fingers pinched his shirt away from his body and he shrugged, sadly, softly.

I remembered how I never enjoyed watching mimes. "You liked sports but not the uniforms?"

He shook his head.

"You liked the uniforms?"

Yes, he nodded, and then he put his hand over his eyes and looked for something sailorwise.

"But you didn't see any?"

What? he said. His mouth clearly said it.

"Look," I said, "how'd you get to be a mute, anyway? I mean, what the hell goes on in that country of yours, anyway?"

His face just fell. Something in me went too. Jesus, what a dumb thing to say. Worse than dumb. At least if you're really truly dumb, your mouth can't rat on you.

That's when I put it together. "You didn't have any uniforms!"

Yes, yes, he nodded. He turned back to the pictures, smiling. They'd been pinned up a while ago but looking at the pictures now surprised me. What my son did with his chest, how he tucked in his chin, ridiculous—and so much like his mother. All at once the pictures dimmed and shifted shape.

My husband's son caught me. His plump cheeks flushed— probably with exertion. I'd lost my footing after all. "I'll tell you something," I heard myself say as I pushed out of his arms, "his dad, *your* dad, he wasn't a fan. I mean he didn't care for sports. No matter how I dressed up our son."

The dogs barked from the backyard. I thought it was my husband at the door, but it was the delivery from the liquor store. My husband's son didn't look like a drinker, but sometimes those people will have a beer with their pizza.

"I promised not to do this," I told my husband's son as he carried the box to the kitchen. "It's not the thrifty way to get liquor into the house."

He began emptying the box, out of some idea of it being a man's job, I suppose. He was taking too long. In a way that he might believe was fairly without interest, I pulled out two fifths I'd ordered for my husband and me. "Either one," I said, "on the rocks."

He took the bottles and set them soundlessly on the counter then relieved me of the ice tray and knife for prying cubes. Did he worry I might hurt myself?

"On the rocks is one of those things that people say." I made conversation to keep from telling him to hurry. "It's from what happens to ships during a storm, isn't it?"

He poured liquor into a glass, adding the ice after. He made the same for himself.

"Let's drink to marriage," I said, "that goes on the rocks." We knocked our glasses together.

"All right," I said, "where'd you learn this language?"

In a shaky hand he wrote on the side of the box that still held some liquor: "I listen."

We knocked glasses on another round. Much of his drink spilled. It was true that he wasn't a drinker because he was drunk now.

"The funny thing about accents," I said, "your father's, yours—I mean, the one you'd have if you . . . Look, people hear them. They say your father still has one. Not directly, no. 'Pardon me,' they say, 'what did you say?' Or they get annoyed. Personally, I don't hear him any more."

My husband's son made wide-eyes and rubbed his flat stomach, letting it be known that he'd need something to eat soon. I refilled our glasses. "I only do this when I'm nervous," I said, handing over his. "Thank you for joining me."

He lifted my hand and kissed it. Now that made me laugh. "So," I said, "what's your best sport?"

He took me in his arms and spun me around. We hit the refrigerator and alphabet magnets flew. Next he led me down the hallway, a narrow hallway, and I'm not a small woman. I expected to hit the wall and was surprised when we didn't. By the living room we made good. There was more space, and he knew some things a dancing partner could do with me.

"Men at one time called me good-looking," I said. His hand wasn't there on the spin and I fell, luckily, onto the couch. "We missed," I said.

When I looked up, my husband, stood in the front door. "You two already started," he said. "I'm glad. I'm glad."

He walked past his son and disappeared into the kitchen. His son wouldn't look at me now. I didn't blame him. I knew what he saw sprawled on the couch, his father's ugly wife. I wanted to assure him there was a time when I was our son's mother. "You're somebody else," my husband said in those years. In those years I was loved and what is loved is not ugly.

My husband strode back in, his hands wrapped around three full glasses. We raised our glasses, and my husband said a toast everyone knows from his language. We grinned and drank fast.

I took the men by their arms and said, "Talk to each other in whatever language feels right. Don't think I mind."

My husband regarded his son. "You look like your mother," he said after a while.

Son smiled at father.

My husband freed his arm from mine in order to pick up the TV remote. We watched him surf channels until he settled on a ballgame. "What's your sport?" my husband said without looking at his son.

His son and I tried not to look at each other. But there was no helping it. We laughed, loud, loud. My husband snapped up the empty glasses and stomped off, no doubt feeling the butt of some joke. From the kitchen he called me. His son didn't look up as I went.

"Why didn't you tell me?" I said as I shuffled into the kitchen.

"Tell you what?" he said. He was pouring himself another drink.

"That your son is a mute."

He lowered his glass. "He can't talk?"

"That's what mute means," I said. "Right?"

He didn't say.

"Well, anyway," I said, "he's still fluent in both languages."

"How do you know?" I had the feeling he was trying to keep up.

"He can hear in both, can't he?"

My husband sat down. "God, what have you been saying?"

"Nothing. We looked at pictures of our son."

"Where'd you find pictures of him?"

I pointed to the stairs, not believing I had to.

He didn't look over there. "Which was his favorite?"

Before me on the counter was a glass. Empty. My empty glass. "It was his mother who called then? I mean to arrange his visit?"

"No," he said, "A relative, a distant one."

"I don't think you told me," I said, pouring myself another, "have you stayed in touch with her, his mother?"

"His mother got on a plane after I left and followed me here. She was pregnant. When she got off the plane, I wanted her like I had in our country. But what was I going to do with her? The authorities put her back on the plane."

"That's not possible," I said.

"I'm telling you she was not allowed in." He swallowed his drink.

I pointed to the box of liquor on the counter. "Look what I did."

My husband pushed up out of his chair and walked carefully to the counter and lifted the lid on the box. "You've got to stop," he said, pulling out another fifth. "It's costing two times as much." Thrift was something my husband could talk about. You could store up a lot with good thrift.

"But why can't your son talk?" I said.

"How the hell do I know?" he said. "I've got nothing to say to that guy out there. I'm glad he can't ask me. I'd give him everything." My husband dropped back into his chair. He shoved his hand over his brow. I pulled his head into my stomach.

We hadn't heard him coming from the living room. Really, we'd not been listening at all for the young man. I think we'd been talking pretty loud. The way drunks talk to each other at street corners.

Over my husband's head I saw again what his son had written on the cardboard box: I listen.

His son stood now in the doorway to the kitchen. My husband got to his feet, pushing me away. He wobbled over to him, laughing, and his son stared at the tears going dry on his father's face. "Sit down," his father said. "Sit down."

The men sat.

His father said, "So here we are . . . Son."

They were going to have a real talk. That's what it was. I should get out of the way. I stepped back too fast, colliding with the box of liquor on the counter and knocking it off. The bottles toppled to the floor, splitting against the tiles and pumping golden liquid.

The young man was up, but my husband yanked him back by the arm. "She'll clean it."

I wanted father and son to talk. That's why I went down to the floor. Must have looked funny though, me on my knees like that, lifting out the big pieces.

"That's something you pick up in a dance hall," I heard my husband say. I could see saying that, for a laugh, even if it really didn't work at that moment.

"It's a joke we have." I stopped cleaning to explain to his son. "Groucho Marx says, 'Here's something I picked up in a dance hall,' and he does an unruly dance. 'Here's something else I picked up in a dance hall,' he says, thumbing over to this big ugly woman, probably his wife."

The young man's hand came to my shoulder then slipped beneath my arm to get me back on my feet.

"Don't," I said.

He hesitated before his hand lifted off me.

I went back to picking up glass but now I was in their way. Both stood. Their arms folded around each other, glass crackling under the soles of their shoes. Dancing is what I thought, maybe a custom between fathers and sons in their country.

This wasn't dancing.

My husband's son was hitting his father in the neck, and my husband was punching back. They had to hug each other tight to get in any good ones. My husband's son was quick and hitting high. My husband managed to dodge a punch to the cheek, but his footwork was no good. He slipped on the wet tiles and went down. Almost as soon as he hit the floor he seemed to swim back up against the wall.

"Get away from me," he hollered at his son, who wasn't coming after him. My husband slapped the counter above him for the telephone. I put the receiver in his hand.

He dialed 911. "There's a criminal in my house!" he yelled into the phone.

The phone was still ringing when I set the receiver back down.

I told my husband's son to go. He stomped out.

There was nothing to putting my husband to bed. He'd worked himself into a chill and welcomed the good comfort. He wanted me to climb in bed with him. I talked instead, which usually causes him to lose interest. I said, "You know, I thought you were dancing with your son. Why would I think that?"

"You see the best in me," he said.

I didn't know my husband's son hadn't left until I went through the living room to lock the front door. He was sitting on the couch in the dark.

I sat down beside him. On the coffee table lay a picture of my son in varsity uniform. My husband's son must have unpinned it from the wall. I said, "This is the last picture we have of him, really. That's as old as he got. I'm not saying our son's dead, you understand. He left. I call him but he doesn't return. He can't even talk to me."

My husband's son pulled out his wallet, where he had his own pictures, all of a slightly older woman that looked like him. I said he could keep the picture of my son in uniform.

My husband's son took my hand in his. His hand seemed smaller, very much smaller, than mine. In that silence between us I heard the wide wounding sound of an airplane circling above. Its lights gone little in so much black sky. Up in that circling plane was his mother heavy with a boy and not allowed in.

INTRODUCTION TO FEATHERS

GUNNER RUN OFF LAST NIGHT AND I'VE BEEN mulling how. He must of had to feather up to fly over the high kennel boards Mother's guy punched up around him not a week ago. If Gunner didn't fly then he squeezed under the boards. There will be no path back to me until I figure out how he got gone.

"It's not how," Mother says. "It's who. Your dog's run off with a family, a farming family, lives on a farm."

Mother is joyful Gunner is gone.

Gunner: bit, made gas, had a mean look. What wouldn't Mother say about my dog?

Such spoil! Gunner scraped and eased nasties right out of the gum and rot off the park's paths by the high-risers downtown: thick manlike hair clippings, pigeons blown open by

dry beans, papers, paper to wipe your ass, a busted bag of doctor pills, once a rubbery worn penis. Gunner would.

But Mother was just scared of looks so filled with beauty.
Gunner's parts you could lay side to side, like gloves behind a
glass counter, the prettiest things made of skin. His eyelashes
stiff as small bones in the clear fins of fish. Pitch-brown hairs
jointed as spider legs out his snout. Gunner was book perfect.
Just look at my book. On front the dog mouths a bird. Inside
all of them brown with eyes. In this book, a dog comes down
to measurements: this thick in the ribs so as to cut through
pond thaw to gather geese shot out of the sky and this wide
across shoulders to haul all that fowl back to you.

This book is where Gunner belongs, not on a farm.

"Your dog can track," the book said. "Your job is to make
him stay on track."

I drew a path in the backyard, flags at one end and sticks
that were the bird Gunner must bring back. Gunner learned
that path easy. Next, I drew on paper a path from the park to
our house so that Gunner could always stay on track to me. I
showed the paper to Gunner. He looked but maybe he didn't
think it was such a good path, after all.

First step, said the book, was introduction to feathers. Start
with dead birds.

In the park, a green-yellow feathery bird fell from a tree,
landing in the wickets of a bush. So death-fresh Gunner run
drunk to it, tenderly soft mouthing it back to me. Right then
I might have kept him on track if only that bird had been his
introduction to feathers. But that fallen fresh green-yellow
bird wasn't Gunner's first. It was another bird. It was Oyster's
rooster.

"Birds perch before a storm," I read the book aloud to Mother. "Smells are stronger before lightening and thunder."

Mother said, "Do you smell stronger before the lightening?"

I couldn't say. Mother and I had not played the smell game since Oyster moved in and put our house in order down to alphabetizing our soup cans, asparagus to vegetable broth.

Oyster strolled in and sat beside where I sat reading. He lifted the book right out my hands. "I've seen this sort of thing," Oyster said. "Dogs used in sports, duck dogs. They don't quit, duck dogs. They find bodies in forests." He kept the book to read on.

"Gunner is one," I said and grabbed back the book.

Oyster looked over quick. "You planning to introduce him to feathers?"

Nobody figured what I was thinking closer than Oyster.

But I wouldn't say.

I wouldn't say how Oyster made his way into my thinking.

He could. Made his way in so much I wondered were my thoughts falling out from my ears? In this way Oyster invaded.

"I got a surprise," Oyster said and he held Mother's and my hand and escorted us to the backyard where he'd staked chicken wire round the eucalyptus, the bark already curling under the wire. Inside the temporary coop stormed a rooster whose black feathers shone round the dumb black pearl eye. His hen already laying eggs. Loose feathers rose and walked out on the breeze, and Gunner snapped at them like a baby catching bubbles, collapsing in a dizzy.

We watched Oyster's rooster strut the yard, its head thrust and beak popped, black tongue poking out at Gunner, Mother, and the trunk of the tree, like he will brawl y'all and lay you flat.

Right then Gunner run straight at the rooster. The rooster skedaddled back behind the floppy chicken wire. But Gunner bowled down the pen and gulped up the bird, shaking it side to side in his soft mouth, white teeth sprouting black feathers. The rooster pecked Gunner's muzzle to bright pins of blood. Three of us circling, Gunner dodging and ducking, bird crowing out his mouth so it was Gunner's mouth that crowed. Until Oyster dove headfirst at Gunner and hooked his arm round the dog's neck, tightening when it bucked and rocking them across the dirt until Gunner spit out that bird to the last feather. The rooster righted itself and tried not to walk crooked back to its hen.

That was Gunner's introduction to feathers.

Then holding his pearl dumb-eyed rooster to his heart like his very own young, Mother's guy told me to rope my dog and not let loose until he had built a dog kennel solid as Alcatraz. Except for a look into my bedroom window, Gunner got gypped out of views owing to Oyster punching up the kennel boards so high.

Meantime, Oyster locked the rooster and hen in Mother's car for safekeeping while he hammered and sawed up a proper coop with walls of fox wire and a private room for brooding. Mother fumed before the door of her car, watching the birds splatter the windows.

We fed on eggs cooked in Mother's frying pan every way an egg can be eaten, so what? When Mother deviled them, Oyster stood up from the table and threw down his napkin, saying he had more appetite for feeding the chickens than feeding himself on such junk. Watering and feeding, Oyster trying his best, every which way he could see.

What Oyster saw in the yellow he gave Mother to peek at. He probably figured that when she saw the bit of blood, she'd want for eggs to hatch.

"How come she's just put out eggs," I said, yoking Gunner to my thigh, "no chicks?"

Oyster looked long at Mother. "A rooster likes his hen to beg."

Eight chicks hatched the very same day my old classmate came visiting with her boy baby. My old classmate had been picked by my schoolgirls as one not to talk to for letting her underpants down and getting a baby started. I had not seen her since she gave up on us and left school and my schoolgirls.

What did anybody need with schoolgirls? There were others to talk to. There was my mother—she hunted babies. Tiny hands, tiny feet, she couldn't do without.

"See how I change him?" Mother undid the baby's pants and pulled out the pisser. "Want to hold it?" she said to me.

Such a thing? I looked out the window, outside to the coop. There was Oyster watering the chicks and stuff.

"Hen had chicks," I said to my old classmate. "When the eggs jittered, Oyster and me, we tapped forks on the shells."

Piss started spraying from her boy baby. Mother, ready your diaper.

I skipped outside.

"Stay with the girls," Mother called after me.

Feathers finer than atmosphere had caught on the wire.

Oyster guided them off with a hose he plugged with his thumb, tempering to a skinny stream. Chicks not too ruffled.

Count chicks, seven in all. All but one hatched out alive. I couldn't tell a chick apart from the next lemon-feathered one. Shteep-shteep. Same is a chick to a chick to a chick. Same is a chick to its mother.

"The hen loves them all," I told Oyster.

"The hen only loves her eggs," Oyster said.

Oyster, how you would talk.

But his talk got me mulling. Was I the same as a chick to my mother? If I got a baby, too, would that make me special? I could feel Oyster's eyes on my thoughts so I flipped subject and said, "Give Gunner a shot at those chicks."

"Things don't come that easy," Oyster said, flooding the ground around the coop, gardening things that don't grow with liquid.

Between slats, Gunner squinted out at the chicks. Clay pots and no flowers was all he had for company. Clip-cleck, clip-cleck was the sound of Gunner walking on clay pots gone to pieces.

"Don't like the way Gunner looks at the chicks," Oyster said. "Only room for one to do that kind of looking."

Bark-bark!

"Yeah?" Oyster sprayed water straight between the slats where Gunner eyed.

Nothing to Gunner. He gulped spray, mouth hung open for more until Oyster took his water on back to the hen. Gunner's tongue flicking up to catch feathers swirling on the hot fog.

Mother's hip knocked open the back door then, and in her

arms was my old classmate's boy baby, his speckled cheeks red with a coming tooth.

"Darling, Oyster," she said, "see this good thing?"

Oyster still had the hose. The hose was still on.

Around the hose he stepped to face her, her on the porch, dress sopped with drool, hair loose and curling under boy baby's chin. Up sneaked the hose and right there, Oyster turned water on Mother, hitting hard at newskin and her. Screams indoors from my old classmate, asking who can she trust with her young?

"Hey, not funny," Mother shouted, twisting jigajig in Oyster's spray.

Oyster's eyes and mouth round with fun.

Boy baby and Mother plowed back inside, water petering out on the door.

Gunner punching barks from his pen.

Oyster dropped the hose to wipe wet hands on his shirt. He knew more than to look at me. Me, holding onto the porch rail, unglued to my nut, laughing. Good thing that wasn't some baby in my arms.

"What's funny?" Oyster said. To cover up how he himself was grinning, he kicked Gunner's boards and the barking stopped.

Mother wasn't in my room. Her perfume was. I could have breathed through it, passed back into sleep through it. The house had filled with her scents before. But her knocking shook me up out of bed.

Mother was knocking on her bedroom door across the hall from mine. "C'mon, precious man," she whispered. "Open up, pearly man." When the knocking stopped, the banging started. Her banging on her door so loud meant I could lift up my window without her hearing. The prints of Gunner's toe pads sweetening my window glass, his to look into, mine to look out.

"Oyster," I heard her say on my way out the window. "Unlock my door. Let me in. Would you lock me out my own room?"

It was a fair jump from a high window. Clay pots crumbled under my feet as I landed. Gunner's kennel smelled of crap somebody had bagged but he tore open. Even this stink was better than what her perfumes did to rooms.

The kennel howled empty. My breath stayed. Where was Gunner?

"Jumped the boards," Oyster said from where he crouched by the coop. Oyster, among the chickens under a haunty-lit moon—not in her room, keeping her out.

Mother, what you didn't know about your Oyster.

"How else he get?" Oyster said, pushing to his feet. "Jumping's the only way."

Downtown's lit risers cast yellow at our eucalyptus tree. Freeway noise drove in our direction. Oyster there by his coop.

"How are the birds? They ok? Did he get 'em?" I said though it was not their welfare I cared about.

Oyster strolled on over to the kennel that now held me in but had not managed to do the same for my dog. "Bright tailed and bushy-eyed," he said, letting an arm drop and swing over the kennel boards.

I dropped my hand over the boards too, feeling for the latch to let me out of the kennel. I aimed to find my dog. But

Oyster lunged across and closed back up the latch. "Only room for one to run off at a time," he said, gone inside my thinking again.

I loosed the latch again and pushed against the kennel door. Hinges whined beneath my hands. "Maybe you think I let him go?" Oyster said, pushing back on the door. "Thinking those chicks are why Gunner made a break for it so how come they're still okay and he ain't?"

"You built his kennel," I said, giving up and backing up to my window, preparing to climb back in. If that's what it took to get out.

"No, it wasn't any puny yellow chicks that Gunner lit out for," Oyster said. On around the kennel he inched, dragging a hand across each slat. Acting like his hand bumping up and down the uneven boards had a mind of its own to fright me. "Maybe you're the one who wanted Gunner gone."

It's quite a fair climb to my window's ledge. I stuck my foot against the kennel boards for leverage. His hand bumped against my arch.

"Maybe he was in the way," Oyster said.

I had a perch on the sill now and might have pulled myself through my bedroom window, but Oyster would of had to let go of my foot first.

The sound of Mother's door burst open from her bedroom. Finally she had found the key. Her bedroom light blinked on, illuminating Oyster before her window. Fingerprints showed up all over her glass now—a mess more than the paw prints Gunner had pressed on mine.

Oyster and me froze, like two rotten bodies caught in the act. Mother flew up the blinds. Eyes blinking blind into the dark out here. Oyster's hand gave my foot a squeeze then lifted off to press against her window glass, adding more finger-prints as he steadied himself for a spy in at Mother.

I could call for Gunner now. Least I could do. My dog might not have got far. But Mother would surely hear. How would she do if she knew Oyster was out here, too, still not answering her?

Or I could run off, like Gunner run off. No room for me in this family. I could beat it to the park. Find Gunner. Show him the path. My body lifted off the windowsill. I rose up and up, tucking under branches. Flying over bags of things, calling soft and not so loud. Calling, Gunner.

"Get on indoors or your dog won't come home," Oyster whispered, fingers pinned to the glass, eyes pearling at Mother's nudity just inches from his face.

"Leave the back door open," he said. "Let her smells out."

I did as Oyster said. I climbed back indoors through my bedroom window. But only to figure out how to hammer and saw a thought-coop tight enough to keep him out of my thinking. Surely I could put up better boards than Oyster built pens.

Cradled, fed, gentled, Oyster did all he could think for the chicks. Second layer of wire, higher posts, driven nails. He made a coop stronghold, knowing things wanted in.

He didn't know how bad.

From below the chicks' feet tunneled squirrels, under-ground workers grabbing for what they could tug between wires. They eased out good things—tiny hands, tiny feet, bits of wing, dragging it all down into the gum and rot. What would not ease through the weave were bodies left for Oyster to gather up in the morning.

Gone, chicks, hen and her black rooster, all gone. But more remains of them than of my dog.

Mother says Gunner found a farm. "Where they raise chickens," she says. "Where they belong."

Your dog can track. Your job is to make him stay on track.

Mother's right. It's not how. It's who.

Duck dog, there's no good path back to me. Go on. Stay away. No room for you here.

Gunner—

THE WORST OF YOU

THEY PICKED HER UP OUT OF THE DIRT in some dear man's turnip patch. Already I'm cute going up in court against some dear man who thinks farming his own is better than paying for it at the grocery where they truck it in packaged. He told the court that she was "sucking dirt off a turnip."

Excuse me?

His lawyer starts in, over and over, saying, "sucking dirt off a turnip." Until I have no choice but to say, "Hey, boys, you getting off on saying this about my little girl?"

And I, Mom, am told to shut up.

Talk turned. It turned to how her dress fit her that day. The dress being too small on her even though she is so skinny down to just ribs. Now I ask you, would I put my little girl in something so tight-fitting when I can *stitch*—alter, seam, sew, everything everything—so if there's one thing she's never gone without it's dresses that fit?

The fit. Think about the fit of that thing they give you to wear *on the inside*—not what I want to think about, but I've got to, got to, until I out-think the thing. See, I got an invite to the big house. Think I ought to accept? What I'm thinking is the big house really ought to be called something else for us, ladies, like the dollhouse. Doesn't that just show where thinking gets you?

I go in the morning so tonight must be for packing.

But what do you pack for a place where the whole point is you don't go out? They do give you those jumpsuits, and, yes, they wash them, but does that get rid of the smell of dollhouse-sized rooms with doors that only lock on the outside?

While I'm on the inside, I can stitch that jumpsuit so the waist's tiny, the pants behave on the ass, and the bust gets up to something. Without a thing to do in the dollhouse except get ready for the man's visit the ladies will pay very good money for that kind of look. I mean every last lady must have money on her? If you're going to take in something, that's something to take in.

Thread is money in the dollhouse. But how much thread do you pack when they said you can only take in one suitcase, this x this small, so even something as thrown-in as thread can occupy importance?

Make room for spools of it.

Get enough money, I bet you can buy your way to certain advantages. Like a one-day visitor's pass for a certain some-body on the outside—they say that in the big house, *on the outside*—but one day of your man friend taking privileges all over you is probably the best you're going to get with stitching no matter how many waists you stitch-in tiny.

All you need is a day. My man was in the next town playing his music with the others. Him so near, I figured I could bus there and back in one day, time enough to get my little girl from my mom's and pull off a dinner. I just wanted to see him. I'd gone before to see him when he was in the next state over and always always got back in time to pull off dinners for my little girl.

I wasn't back in time this time. That's how come my little girl wandered next door to the dear man's turnip patch. Since my mom wasn't around, I'd left her a little something of something in the back of the refrigerator, but my little girl gets worried. That's when she might do anything, wander out of the house even. Who can blame her, I don't. She doesn't have much appetite. I mean she's skinny, and them saying you could see her ribs made me look like I didn't keep her in food. It just happens that you *can* see her ribs because she takes after me, Mom, I'm skinny.

Ladies at the dollhouse will take this into account when making up their minds about paying for my stitching. They won't all look so good as I do skinny no matter how much thread I use. So there's probably more to think about than the fit.

There's these papers to think about, as example.

Pretty soon I have to write my name on them, but it doesn't mean I have to read them. Put me in the dollhouse and take away my little girl but you can't make me read those papers. Let my mom read them. She's probably reading them now.

My mom used to care about my heart. So long as it took

only one day for me to get to my man friend and back. My mom and my little girl, they'd eat together. Eating is something with my mom. She's the one gave me the food tied up in a tablecloth to make like a picnic for him. "The fastest way to a man's heart is through his stomach." That's what made me think she cared, but thinking on it now I should not have taken the heart-through-the-stomach advice as caring. In the first place it wasn't *my* heart she was caring about. In the second, you don't say something that's been said so many times it's just something to put on paper. Paper that says my little girl is no longer mine, she's my mom's now, is all she's going to have on me, but I can visit.

Will that mean she's also got to, under the law, take my little girl to see me in the dollhouse? Hey, I have to tell my little girl about that name dollhouse so when she visits she'll think how it's a treat for her doll, too. The dresses that doll's got, you should see them. The details like love bits. I've stitched beads, sequins, buttons and broidery on those little dresses. I'd do the same for my little girl's own wear, but she likes her dresses off the rack, store bought, like the girls at school wear so I hunt up dresses at seconds and take them in, a stitch here, a tuck there, no darts, no pleats, nothing much, simple, so nobody can tell, and she wears them happy. With the doll's dresses it's no stops. Flashy, the more the more. A little shop of doll dresses is what we're hanging out a sign above someday, just us two. Already I'm teaching her stitching. That's why my little girl says she'll never go away from me, and I say oh, you can go all right, but leave the doll, and that gets a big ha ha.

Can't you see all the ladies getting a big ha ha out of my little girl bringing her doll to the dollhouse? No, they won't laugh at that, I mean not if you think about it. They'll be too busy *trying to get* laughs out of their own little girls and little boys who come to visit for maybe twenty minutes out of a day that goes on for twenty-four hours that don't end.

Those visits, the little girls' and little boys' ones, they're a different fit. They're a Mom fit. For that the ladies will want stitching that makes you look like Mom. This look isn't tight. This is letting out the seams, making room—holding room for the little ones.

A stitch in time will save my ass in the dollhouse. The ladies will pay one visit to be good-looking for the man. The next visit to look like Mom. Two different fits. She's only got the jumpsuit to wear, and it'll need to be let out and taken in, let out, taken in. Hear it? My man friend calls it talking with your ear. It wants music.

And maybe that bothered him. But the fact was I needed a good amount more than an hour to take in the dress for his back-up singer. Sewing it up meant using a stitch that could come unstitched easy so that the dress, a rental, could go back the next day. An hour was all I had.

You free up a man's time, he thinks about fucking. Not so with the ladies, not so. Without a man around to keep her mind on a tight fit, she starts thinking about being Mom. How she is a Mom or she should be a Mom or how she is going to become a Mom first thing she does when she's *on the outside*. That's why a man's such a good fuck and why one who remembers he's got a kid runs the risk of not being such a good one.

Some ladies do get their minds free of the Mom thing long enough to think about fucking. Some of them even go for it.

I mean, some do. Those ladies are tough, people who've done crimes. Their faces hang in pictures in places strangers go. I saw my face in a gas station. It was one in a row of pictures below some ill-fitting words, one of them was *child neglect.* I couldn't picture it. I don't think the boys working the gas station put the two together, either. Not because the picture made me look fat—thank you, Mom, for supplying police with that particular snap—but because you just don't. There was my photograph in a gas station, but I am not tough.

Baby, I stitch. That's something every lady will know the minute I open my suitcase, all the thread. That says if in the dollhouse you want the clothes good fitting, you had better not be cute with me. Though all that thread may say something else to the guards. They may not take so kindly to spools of thread since wherever there's thread there are needles. Needles are probably a big no-no at the dollhouse; if there's one tiny item that has about as many wrong uses as right ones, it's a needle. Needles might even be on the list of things you can't take in—that list is in the other stack of papers I've been meaning to read—but somewhere along the dollhouse corridor, somebody is going to get fed up with tripping over her unhemmed jumpsuit and start hollering out for needles. *Sewing* needles, that is, and who's got anything against those?

Nobody. Nobody, and neither do I. Since we're declaring ourselves here, I might as well add that I am not against ladies doing each other, either. It's playing dolls. That's why they call it the dollhouse. In there the ladies could be doing it regular as dolls. I've got to tell my little girl about that. Not about the ladies doing like dolls, not that. I've got to tell her to come visit me. Calling it a dollhouse will help.

I'll tell her now.

It's an hour before check-in at the dollhouse, time enough to go over to Mom's and tell this to my little girl. I thought I wasn't done packing my suitcase but now that it's all a matter of thread, well. Time I got.

Or do I? The thing of it is, what I'm thinking is, if I'm going all the way over to Mom's to talk to my little girl, I might as well just take my little girl with me. Not to the dollhouse, oh no, she can't get on the inside.

Underground. That's where we'll go, underground.

Watch us go.

I think this is exactly what I was after the whole time I was packing. But I kept thinking about what to pack for going in the dollhouse instead of what to pack for *not going*.

My suitcase's packed, maybe with too much thread now, but there's no time to unpack thread. I'll take the suitcase into Mom's house. Sure, my mom may have posted bail so I could come home and get things in order, but she won't let me inside her house now if I don't look like I'm on my way out of her life. I'll bring the papers, too. While she's looking for my sign-away on the dotty line, I'll tell my little girl we're going.

"The next time you see your little girl," Mom said, "it'll be through bars." That was after the time in court where the lawyers kept talking on about the turnip. I told my mom right then it was part her fault. I said, "If you'd taken care of her like I asked, none of this would of happened."

"I told you the last time," she said, "was the last time."

Okay, the truth is—I don't have time anymore to make sure everybody's looking good in the picture—my mom is a witch if ever one rode a broomstick overhead.

I said, "Who needs you, Mom?" I said other things, too. When your whole life is one of being thankful to a witch, it feels good to finally let a little out.

Then my man friend called and said, "Are you the best fuck? I can't remember."

Like I said, I left my little girl back in the refrigerator a little something of something to eat, saying baby don't leave the house, Mom's got stitching to do and will be back in twenty-four. That was better than saying my man friend doesn't like kids around so he knows nothing about you.

No more telling stories to my little girl after we go underground. We'll take on new names and she'll start new at school. I can always earn something from stitching. More doll dresses is what she'll ask for, so I'll teach her the finer points—I really will now no more losing patience with how her fingers jump the needle wider and closer never regular—and when the stitching isn't paying we'll maybe lift from the grocery, and she'll like that because the last I caught her with lifted candy hidden in her underwear I really really walloped her, not something she liked but lifting's not right did she want to be wanted by the law?

Did she?

Did she?

The law will be wanting a thing or three with me for not showing up at the dollhouse and instead going underground with my kid that I'm supposed to be signing away to Mom, and that's okay with me. Move over biggest fuck-ups. I've out fucked-up the worst of you.

The being-the-best-fuck part, that's—well, I'm thinking now that really means how much you love. God's truth, and I was trying to tell that to the courtroom, but who wanted to listen to how I was up six nights stitching and unstitching rented dresses and on night seven no rest because the man friend needs reminding of me in the biblical sense so when it came to stitching my own little girl's dress I'd, by the mistake of pure tiredness, done a stitch that could come unstitched easy easy, you've seen thread, how it unspools, that's how my mouth was going—

"Truth?" the lawyer said. "Haven't heard a word of it."

His lawyer saying that about my little girl's dress. How when police got to the turnip patch—it wasn't anything that dear man had done, one look at him and you'd know not him, never him—they saw how she wore it. The dress, in other words, wasn't. Undone, unstitched, slipped down, no dress, naked, as the day, my little girl.

The bottom line truth about being Mom is that you ought to let your little one in, *on the inside.*

You take something in, you got to let something out. Basic sewing.

I'm not that tough baby, I told you.

I take something in, I got to let something out, so what's to stop it from coming out and coming out and coming out—

WHAT'S TO LIGHT?

H E SEES THAT THING-THERE'S EYES LIT UP WITH flashlight and what the old man says is, You'd scare an old dark creature like that?

He scares me worse, I say.

Don't you know, he says, you got to let some things stay in the dark.

The old man acts like that thin-skinned thing's had its fill of me, but it's not of me. Didn't I see the creature lying belly up in the filed, getting dressed by the old man's quick hands that don't rush, finger-walking along and lifting skin? No way some strange hand's getting in that thing-there's belly. Before the old man could make the coat, the creature flipped back onto all fours and raced off a field that was for it just a fitting room where what's discarded was a hide.

Do you remember, I say to the old man, that time in the field?

I had it down to a carcass, he says.

That one's carcass ran off on you, I say.

Sometimes, he says, the dead have got more life to live than the living. Cut the light, he says.

My light's beam holds steady in the thing-there's eyes, unsettling it little. It sorting through the trash of our garbage that lids bones and skins made crispy in the old man's skillet.

Take him to bed, he says, or shoot him, girl.

The banister swings out with the old man, like some kind loose armature, loosening from too many climbs up stairs without truly wanting to get up top. He will not listen, like Mother listened, for my steps to pass along the hallway, and she only listening because fretting was her what. Big girl, she hollered from behind their door, moon fix you to that porch?

Now the old man sleeps full on in darkness that shutters blinds and curtains, going deaf to all sound, excluding of that one, the noise of her.

This is no noise that comes to my ear or any other's. This is a noise that only he can listen for in sleep. Didn't hear a thing, I have to keep saying to him.

And the old man keeps saying back, It's how your mother comes to me. You would like it somehow fancier?

What a racket makes that thing-there behind Zorro's mask. Shunk and dunk, a dance on tin. I can shine up eyes and gain no greater climb than a flea, one of so many vermin that hound that thing-there's hide. Accustoming to my flashlight, it lifts a bone, borrowing the light to inspect the sort of meat that still clings. Higher, higher it must stretch, going way up on its hinds to reach my light that's raised in trickery for a peek at its belly. Tilt the wrist, and the light locates it, the erupture there that is the old man's what. This is where the old man started to roll up skin, carpet like, and the last thing separating that thing-there from the entire world was one sheety membrane that didn't just hold innards in but kept out the wants of the world, too.

A membrane don't let bleed, big girl, said the zoo's new keeper that night. The shell don't give up the yolk.

Less it gets a cracking, I said when he called on me uninvited.

Hic-up. He made that sound again and again that night.

The new keeper took me for any dumb creature, but I was seeing blood. Flashlight showed it dotting the inside of my legs well before the keeper had done the wiping up with chickeny napkins from the garbage.

This was my erupture, stayed in the hiddenest carcass of me.

Hear the creak and ease of the stairs, the old man has come back down, one step a time in a tread that's cousin to sleep-walking. I blacken my light. Next, I stretch out bellywise on the boards, hiding low, hoping that thing-there in the tree has the same sense to quiet. No such luck with the mockingbird tooting from the tallest pine. There is no end of song in a courting bird, the old man says. Variety is all that counts.

Mother has caused the old man to relinquish his no-embrace and rise from his bed once again. It's her noise he must be hearing, as she pivots in all directions of the night, calling, What, Mina, what?

The front door swings open and the porch night appears

wholly milky against the old man, who is letting Mother know this: Don't fuck with me, Mina.

In this full walk of sleep, the old man is blind to me laid out flat as I am, and his heel grinds strands of my hair into the boards as he stumps off. Gone this time, again for some unknown time. Mother has a hold on the old man that never held so tight when she lived. When she lived, the cries of the hungry zoo animals roused only her before daylight—even as the smell of oats and cinnamon steamed up from the kitchen through the floorboards, circling our heads, our faces pressed into pillows, us willing away the light of a day that for Mother was more than half done.

Gone, too, is that thing-there. With my flashlight I browse through what remains of the sorry picnic the creature has left on our porch. I ought to tidy up a bit. But then sleep comes over, now that night brings on the dawn, and dawn the daylight in which the new keeper dare not venture. Come daylight the zoo requires keeping.

I hear footsteps on the front porch, but none of the old man's weight in those steps.

Your father left you like this? my mother's sister calls out. There's shame in this sight. Aunt lifts me up and up I go from the porch floor, opening my eyes while keeping the lids shut, playing a game on daylight.

She props the wall behind my back, and I make glad use of it, collecting my what to face the day. Aunt turns fierce upon the sorry picnic I failed to tidy. This I hear in clanky tins and rattlesome bones. I open my eyes and see that I am right in picture listening. Aunt has redeemed our front porch for us, removing the innards from view. Always like this, is Aunt. She is jangly after a night's work keeping her eyes on things at the zoo.

Aunt slaps the flashlight into my palm and points with a push at my shoulder toward the old man's bathroom and the sound of pounding water filling the tub. It's Aunt's zoo flashlight, made a gift to me for when the old man leaves me alone at night. I step over the rim of the tub. Water rises up my thighs as I lower down.

I shine the flashlight beam on Aunt's chest, but it has no punch, everything being touched by daylight. Aunt sees what I am at and screws off the bulb over the toilet and draws down the shade, pushing day's light back on itself. I glide the light beam over the water. The beam races in to fill the picture of thighs drowning.

See what-all there is that swims in and out between my legs, I say.

Aunt's hands lower into the water and draw my thighs gently closed. Aim at night foulers, Aunt says. But shoot with light.

He take his wallet this time? Aunt says, water running off her fingertips.

Every joker around here knows the old man, I say. He will find his way back home.

It's not his whereabouts I worry over, Aunt says. Without his wallet, how am I to manage you a plate of food? Feed the animals? Pay the bills? The debtors are hungry.

She hurries out the bathroom, to look for the old man's wallet, I reckon. The old man says Aunt is see-through, glass of water, especially on those occasions when she's drying out. But I hear Aunt has a few tricks, especially with all that's words. She pens up snappy signs for the zoo, things to remember for some day, things to read aloud like: *Go hog wild and root for the Zoo's cutest porcine. Isn't it time you had something to snout about?*

A suck and a swirl, water quiets on the drain. That's when I hear a noise.

Click-click.

A silvery comb against porcelain.

Crack it on my forehead. Yellow ball and fishy gel slide down my scalp. Egg to remove snarls, Mother says. Vinegar to bring back shine.

What all passed through the comb stayed around to clog the drain.

The old man covering up his mouth after getting a whiff of me, Mother's vinegar and egg detangler gone rotten on a head sweating in full-sun.

Click-click. Click-tap.

This noise is new to the house.

I go find Aunt.

The click-tap at my ears follows me into the old man's room. A room seethy with tobacco and dark enough for my flashlight's beam to guide lighthouse steady across Aunt, who is spread out, butter across bread out, among the old man's possessions. Green bottle glass shining ruby in her hand. Her dress hiked up so her belly floats above the world. My light golds the hairs that bunch at her drawers, hairs sprouting like worn broom, though Aunt is not near so old as the old man. In the glare of her belly shines a blood centipede stitched to the skin there after some strange hands must have got in. Aunt has kept her secret in tight. But guts, they don't lie. The blood centipede there is nothing but my aunt's very own eruption.

Aunt's open mouth sucks in air, blows it out, a pig's sleep. She does not hear what begins again in my ear.

Click-click. Click-tap.

The silvered sound so near my ears untangles the hair. I will not now cry the tears I would not cry from a comb that touched not mercy, only scalp.

Is this the same noise the old man hears? Or does Mother court us each with our own song? Perhaps variety is all that counts, even for the dead.

I hood the light's beam with my hand. My palm's fortune burns orange. This noise is up—this noise is wide—I train my light beam on Aunt and gunslinger-back out of the old man's room. Thinking this-there noise is not my expertise. This is *his* noise that only he ought to have to listen for. Thinking the old man missed Mother's living life, can he fail to attend the haunting?

I hightail it out of the house.

The sun winks out behind the far line of pines. The day's lost red. Still the old man. Well, he has not returned.

The new keeper has. His eyes swelling in dusk light, he stands before the porch steps. Your aunt around? he says.

I shrug.

Go in and tell her to come out, he says.

Might be she's sleeping, I say. Then I sit down on the top porch step.

He stuffs both hands in the pockets on back of his denim. Pants already tight.

Wake her, he says. Hic-hup. His fist to his lips but never a Pardon me.

Next minute, night's back on.

The new keeper lays the heel of his boot on the bottom step. Your aunt, he says. Go on in and ask when she last paid the electric.

Go in yourself, I say.

Zoo's dark as a ape's ass, he says. The problem's not with light, he says. Beasts don't mind a little night. But the incubators, they cold up.

It's about time you had something to snout about, I say.

The new keeper leans in and runs a hand over my scalp. Oh, he says, so, why won't you go in your own house?

Noises, I say. Switching on Aunt's flashlight, I use it like a hand shove at his chest. I say, There might even be a noise in there for you.

Noises, he says, his boot jerking off the bottom step. Hooding his eyes from the light, he backward-walks out the yard.

House is dark, settling around Aunt in there as I settle down to listen for the old man. The mockingbird starts up again, manufacturing a click-tap sound for variety. I am gratified when a ruckus in the closest pine shuts up that bird. Shine light on branches and the thing's there, a zig-zag striped crook crawling up a pine branch ladder. Grey feathers float out its snout.

I switch off my flashlight.

Leave the thing-there to its old dark business.

Allow a little night.

Old man prefers the dark. So what's to light in his return?

NOT. IN NOTTINGHAM

WHILE MY HOSTESS SAT ACROSS THE GLASS KITCHEN table fanning away the smell of diarrhea exploding from one of two recently adopted kittens mewling on the other side of the screen door, while my six-year-old son, also on the other side of the screen door, finally took the turn he'd never been offered to mount his friend's toy arrow in a bow, while the boy he'd come to play with, the boy named after the Hindu principal of cosmic order, abandoned my son in favor of his brother, I began wondering why I'd agreed to take a kid like mine on a playdate.

Eddie stepped up to the screen door and said, "Mom, what would it be like to be unaffected?"

"Where'd you hear a word like that?"

Unaffected was a funny word for a kid to use, even for Eddie. Was he asking if things would be different if he hadn't been hurt as a toddler, if so much of life since hadn't been taken up with recovery: ICU, long-term hospitalization, surgeries, learning to walk again, ongoing psychotherapy? Was he asking what it would be like if he could just take whatever life threw at him without ducking? Or was it a bid for protection in this, if not hostile, sort of negligent environment? Eddie shrugged then poked the toy arrow at the tiger striped kitten, which batted it enthusiastically.

"Where's your friend?" I said.

"He doesn't want to play with me," he said.

My hostess, a woman of marmalade disposition from Orange County, slid open the screen door, slipped past Eddie and padded out to the kitty litter clumping in a box beside the door.

Eddie stared through the screen at the kitchen table dotted with serving platters of organic wheat currant scones, edamame, and a cheese substitute made of almonds, all snacks he'd refused. "Find your friend," I said. "Say goodbye." He could be polite even if his friend wasn't.

Grace Loh-Huntington, raking litter in tailored hippie chic, said, "Isn't he upstairs with his brother?" She said it like we would know.

I held the screen door open for Eddie, not the kittens—Grace wanted them outdoors with their diarrhea—then trailed after him. Just off the kitchen there was a stairway with wide, wide steps, wide like the rest of the house that spread over two lots a block west of the bluffs above Santa Monica beach, where a personal trainer militia trolled for the out of shape. Eddie trudged up the white carpeted steps without looking back.

My hostess had not offered to show me around the sunny living room, sunny dining room, or sunny family room that flowed out the kitchen and into one another like a river of gold. Why no curtains on the windows? Perhaps there was nothing to hide. Of particular note was the number of coffee tables dispersed through the rooms. Coffee tables were a sore spot in my marriage. My husband called them the sacrificial altar of the living room, so we'd never owned one so it was never comfy in our living room so friends and family rarely gathered there. How could I make him understand that the locus of family is in the coffee table? Perhaps it was a Russian thing, decrying coffee tables, but my Russian émigré husband was not *that* Russian. He never spoke it and avoided the company of those who did.

Bathroom, pantry, stocked liquor cabinet, and a linen closet, thoughtful with plush towels and spare racecar toothbrushes for sleepovers; all this peeking without my hostess' permission was making me a spy. Besides, Eddie had been gone so long I was starting to wonder if he'd been made to feel welcome. Full of hope, I headed back through the living room to the kitchen and my hostess. Time to lighten up, maybe crack a few jokes. Hear about the kitten that lost all her money? Now she's *paw*.

What I saw through the kitchen screen door was my son taking off his tunic. Though by no means his only costume, he'd come to this particular playdate dressed as Robin Hood. But how had Eddie returned to the backyard when I'd watched him go upstairs? In spite of my self-guided tour, all spatial sense of the house slipped away, as if this very moment, behind my back, the entire house was rearranging itself, a device to punish snoopers.

The sound of children's laughter wafted up from the street. Perhaps the Loh-Huntington boys had not gone upstairs as their mother suggested but out to play with the neighborhood kids. How isolating our home seemed in comparison. My son was more likely to bump into a rattlesnake than a neighbor boy. We didn't live in a neighborhood. We lived in a remote canyon. My husband said he needed to write without being disturbed. He now locked himself in his studio at night, pulling the curtains on the glass doors, the same glass doors where by some accident of light and reflection songbirds kept breaking their necks. Sergei had taken to lining up the dead birds like casualties of a firing squad. I anticipated coming across the weightless hapless things to find little pieces of cloth tied across their eyes.

That must be how my son had returned to the backyard; he'd run down another staircase, into the foyer, then out the front door and around back. That is, if he hadn't taken some other route. What kind of a protector was I if I couldn't keep track of his comings and goings? One thing was certain; the bow and arrow were a big draw. There was no denying Eddie had a feeling for accessories. His green felt hat lay at my feet.

As part of our leave-taking, I knelt beside Grace and her sun-kissed thighs so toned in her shorty short shorts it struck me that pet care could be sexy. She raised watery eyes to me. The litter raking was getting to her. Her baby was sick. Why make light of it? Hadn't I often wished I had the kind of a life that could keep a pet, any pet, even a cricket? A cricket was good for your conscience.

Grace frowned at the green hat in my hand then squinted at me without comprehension.

"Eddie loves Robin Hood. You know, steal from the rich, give to the poor."

Grace said, "Who said that?"

I laughed and looked over at Eddie, who was tap dancing on the pool concrete and singing "Not in Nottingham."

"Yeah," I said, "I don't think all that 'Let's put on a show' makes Eddie very popular."

"Dar's teacher says he's the most popular boy in first grade," Grace said. "She told us to be on the look out for signs of stress."

It took a minute before I figured out she meant *her* son, which meant *my* son's first grade. Then I put it together. Dar was a nickname for her son, and this playdate was just one more stressor for Dar. A wonder that their teacher had orchestrated it in the first place. I guess Dar's emotional equilibrium was worth taxing in the name of elevating Eddie from playground skid row; after all, this was Eddie's first playdate this year. I continued to do the calculations. If Dar was the most popular boy in the class then that made his mother the reigning queen, and if raking kitty litter and ignoring the fact that your offspring blows off his guest was the gold standard of mom-playdate conduct, then I could learn from this woman.

"My husband Sergei's book *Mistakes of Memory*—his first— just won a prize from the Modern Language Association. It's about Stalin's terror," I said.

"Oh, terror's good."

"I think my husband is a Russian spy," I said. "He complains the award makes him feel like an imposter. No wonder. He's never written anything before in his language. Or ours.

All the while we've been married, he's been a sleeper cell. He's been activated."

Ripping into a bag of cat litter, Grace said, "You hear of cases like that."

Obviously I was joking about the Russian spy thing. The idea had come to me in her kitchen. But lookee here, Grace was up to tricks, game for a bit of *what if?* "That reminds me of a story," I said. "This charming guy says to the woman he's about to get involved with, 'One day I'll have to kill you, but this is interesting, what we've got going between us here. This thing you're doing, it's good.' So what do they do? They get married. They have a kid. Struggle. Overcome challenges. You know the drill. Then on the very morning they feel most in love, the charming guy says, 'I will have to kill you.' "

Eddie's cool hand yanked my forearm. He wanted to show me that the arrow had lost its suction cup. Now it was just a stick that someone had whittled to a sharp point.

I said, "Be careful with it, Eddie."

"My kids make me jumpy, too," Grace said.

Whoa, Grace, nobody said anything about jumpy. Time to clear up a few things. First of all, my husband was the one who told me that story, way back when we were dating. Guess the story was on my mind because he'd just sort of hinted at it again. On the fridge, on the chalkboard for making lists, for all the world to read, he'd written: *Tomorrow morning: kill MOM.*

"The story is about how you fool yourself into believing you've met the real deal, but really the only deal going is the one you've cut with him," I said. "It's like being Scheherazade. Every marriage has an expiry date."

Grace said, "We were married in Kauai."

Okay, so she was not paying attention. She was rubbing a kitten's belly. And really, what did she need to know about it, this little routine between my husband and me? It was true that in our 19 years of marriage, even in the midst of our fall-out over Eddie's accident, Sergei had yet to say anything about killing in the morning. In fact, the meaning of the message on the fridge was much simpler. Sergei was referring to his book, *Mistakes of Memory*, for which MOM was an acronym. It was the book that he planned to kill. Hadn't he said it made him feel like an imposter? Perhaps that's also how marriage had come to feel to the man who one day kills his wife.

"Has your husband ever said he'd have to kill you, Grace?" I said.

"Every time he opens a credit card bill," said Grace, turning to watch Eddie fly the arrow across the swimming pool gentrifying the back yard. Good thing his archery was all theater. The arrow soared over the head of a blow-up Buddha to thwick in the ornamental grass clipped shabby on the other side. Nothing good was going to come of Eddie shooting an arrow honed to a point. As he sped around the pool for it, I hustled after him. Time to face facts. My hostess and I had nothing in common. But as I shoulder-punted Eddie to within an inch of the water, I knew that if I accepted this, I had to accept a whole lot of desolation. Grace had been a good sport to take on the playdate. No need to take on our pain, too. Pain isn't a favor you do somebody. Didn't she have enough worries with her sickly kitten? She'd adopted the kittens for her boys' pleasure and now, look at the mess; what we do for our boys. I landed the bow and arrow on a bright striped towel stacked on a high glass shelf.

"Can I pour you a drink?" I said when I got back. "Don't mind if I do with that booze bar of yours."

"I never touch the stuff." Grace stood up and tied a plastic bag sagging with spooned-out diarrhea.

"Do you have any hobbies?"

"No."

While Eddie, with invisible arrow drawn on invisible bow, stalked the white kitten, I said, "That's right, Mama. Who's got time for hobbies? It takes every spare minute to just keep up with dietary trends." Judging by those healthy and sophisticated snacks for the kids, she knew a thing or two.

Grace strode round to the side of the house lined with trashcans. I was right on her heels, but she stepped back with a look that said, give me a little space, okay? Then she raised the bag between us and pointed to the blue/green/brown trashcans framed by grasping bougainvillea. "Recycle, compost, or garbage?"

"Throw it into your neighbor's yard," I said.

She slung it into the compost, which seemed cavalier, but then I wasn't a composter. Garbage disposals still transfixed me. The sick kitten slunk past.

She snatched it up. Arms extended, she strode back around the house. Brown dribbled down the kitten's lank white legs.

On the other hand, maybe I was a composter. Recycling the old marriage tropes just wasn't cutting it. In other words, my husband wasn't the only one who felt like an imposter. I'd been faking the mom-thing for a while now. True, every mom at one time or another housed a sick kitten, but that mom could rely with confidence upon her motherly intuition to do the right thing. When it came to Eddie, my intuition was a busted clock, lucky to be right twice a day. Since my imper-sonation of a mom was no longer sufficient to the task, maybe MOM did need to be killed off, or at least composted. Could some new being rise up from the alluvial soil to mother Eddie?

Recycle, compost, or garbage. There was another option—throw Mom in the garbage, but then who'd take the kid to birthday parties?

Picking my way through the grass, I said, "I didn't see you at Jimmy's birthday."

"So many parties," Grace said. "We went to Seraphina's birthday gig instead."

"Since you missed, I'll fill you in. Jimmy's entire backyard was covered in mini racetracks." This was the only birthday party Eddie had been invited to, so we'd shown up. "Young men stationed at each table helped the kids operate the slot cars. Eddie was having nothing to do with the slots."

"The doctor gave me medicine for the kitten. Did you see the dropper anywhere?"

No, I did not see the dropper. "A couple parents pulled their eyes off the slot cars long enough to ask what was up with Eddie," I kept on. "I told them Eddie was just weak from the fumes."

"The doctor said parasites." The kitten was hiccupping in tiny chokes. Grace hurried to the screen door.

"I thought maybe some parent would run with the slot car *bon mots* but all I saw were taillights," I called after her, hear-ing myself.

Eddie stood on the other side of the screen door. When my hostess slid it open, he did not step out of her way.

"Can I hold the kitty?" he said.

Grace looked over her shoulder at me, like she didn't speak Eddie.

"Can he?" I pantomimed cradling.

She shook her head. "He's going back to the vet." She said it like Eddie was going back to the vet, like Eddie was an animal. As Grace inched around Eddie, who didn't budge, his hand feinting at the sick kitten held out of reach, she screamed.

I pushed between Eddie and her into the kitchen.

Side by side on the bottom step of the kitchen staircase hovered the two brothers, materialized out of the ether like cherubs, except instead of an arrow poised to launch, the younger held his hand over his eye, an arrow sticking out it. Red ran down his cheek.

Grace gaped at her son. "Dharma. Oh god, oh my god."

"Eddie shot him," said his brother. His eyes flashed at me.

Eddie started to shake. I knew the signs and grabbed his arm before he could bolt. Then I marched him over to Dharma.

Dharma backed away from us. "Mom! I lost my eye!"

"Get him away from Dharma!" Grace sprung at Eddie, hauling him by his shoulders off her son. In the mean time, I plucked out the arrow from between Dharma's fingers, spun round, and presented it to Grace.

Grace stared at the arrow in my hand then at Dharma, whose intact eyes shone bright as he glanced sideways at his brother. He guffawed.

Grace relaxed her grip, hand hovering over Eddie's shoulder for a moment before coming back down for a quick pat. Her eyes did not meet mine as she gave back my son. Turning to the sink, she reached for the paper toweling and soap. While

Dharma wiped the ketchup he'd used for blood from his cheek, while the kitten, growing thinner by the second, meowed at her feet, Grace worked her hands into a good lather.

"You'll have to excuse us." She looked at me now. "We wait any longer, the vet's office will close." She turned to her boys. "Get in the car."

Eddie watched them go, his eyes faintly ringed with blue.

"Bye, Eddie," Dharma called from the door then chucked the paper toweling onto a coffee table.

"Bye," Eddie said.

Dharma's brother sprinted after them, hollering, "Mom, where's my bow?"

"In the trash?" she said.

"Recycle, compost, or garbage?"

Sergei's car wasn't in the driveway when we got home, and I was relieved not to cook beyond toaster oven. Faced with a plate of chicken nuggets, Eddie clasped his throat, choking-on-bone style, and poured himself onto the floor under the dinner table. After subsiding into pajamas, he rifled through his costume box until I lowered the curtain and cut the lights, bedtime.

Outside, a sharp crescent moon illuminated nothing. The beam from my flashlight swung across the path to Sergei's studio at the edge of our woods. The glass door wasn't locked, but the place was a cave. So much for the shorty short shorts I'd changed into just for Sergei. He wasn't there. As I stepped back, some brittle thing popped beneath my heel. I snatched up my foot and shone the light on the stoop, expecting the line of birds. The birds were still there, the line wasn't; they'd had been scattered, wings that had been tucked in, penguin style, were now spread open as if for crash landings. One bird was pretty much decapitated. At first I thought bobcat, but desiccated songbirds seemed such meager fare. That left Eddie. He must have done it after we got back. Maybe he blamed them—something had caused his parents to stop speaking to each other, why not little dead birds? But did he have to decapitate?

Morning was a long way off, so was sleep, so I treaded back into Eddie's room. Round cheeks, open mouth, high light breath, Eddie's peaceful slumber should have reassured. He let out a little cry, turned his back to me, and the blanket fell away. Apparently, he'd sneaked downstairs and changed because he now wore the Robin Hood costume. The short tunic exposed his legs and the scars there, thanks to the car accident that had nearly killed him.

When did Eddie have time to rough up the birds? There hadn't been enough between dinner and bed. Could it be he didn't do it? Might have been anybody. All this not-knowing was jitter-making. Where was Sergei? This was the kind of thing a man should be home for.

My mistake was agreeing to the playdate. Someone once said, more or less, that it's immoral to act against your own intuition. I wasn't the only one who had. Grace obliged her kid's teacher and hosted a child she believed in her gut capable of shooting an arrow into her kid's eye. Was it Grace's fault she had kitten-sized empathy? That she lacked the emotional equipment for a playdate with PTSD?

Midnight had come and gone. Time to unfurl bologna for Eddie's bag lunch. Across the darkened kitchen, the refrigerator loomed like a headstone. Behind the door a plastic bottle of ketchup splatter stood on its head. I slammed shut the refrigerator door, penduluming Sergei's note. *Tomorrow morning: kill MOM.*

Guess Sergei's book-burning campaign was still set for the morning. And why not? Didn't Grace say terror's good? But then again, maybe he really meant it: kill MOM, me, Eddie's mother, tomorrow morning, which was today. Now, in fact.

Footsteps creaked overhead. A light came on in the hallway. It was still dark enough for Eddie to throw a shadow across the staircase. He held a bow in his hands.

The telephone rang. I jumped. A hush focused the next ring.

I grabbed the phone. "Hello?"

"It's Grace."

"Hi?" I said.

"I thought you should—" Grace hiccupped. "Should know. The kitten didn't—"

"I'm so sorry," I said.

"By the time we got to the vet's . . ."

"Dead?"

"*Dead,*" Grace slurred. The smell of booze came over the line.

From the tail of my eye I saw a grappling with an arrow. At least that's how it seemed. I didn't want to look. Behind my back there was a commotion, a tensing on that invisible line that attached us.

"Yeah, well," she said, fumbling the receiver. "I never even wanted cats."

"Grace, wait," I whispered. "Please. Don't hang up."

ACKNOWLEDGMENTS

Heartfelt thanks to the staff at University of Massachusetts Press. Deep gratitude to Amy Hempel and to the Association of Writers and Writing Programs.

I'd also like to offer my thanks to the editors at the literary journals and anthologies who stick by the short story in all its forms, including but never only: John Colburn, Kevin Prufer and Susan Steinberg, Michael Koch, Matthew Cooperman, Aurora Brackett, the unswerving Ronald Spatz, Jim Clark and Steve Almond, Bill Henderson, Sarah Shute and Mimi Davis, Melanie Bishop, Nigel Hinshelwood, Randa Jarrar, and Linda Swanson-Davies and Susan Burmeister-Brown.

To those who asked more of each word, John Rechy, Tom Filer, Lou Mathews, Gordon Lish, Pinckney Benedict, and Joanna Scott, who also gave faith and kept giving. Thanks to Sandra Loh, to Michelle Latiolais, to Alexis Seely. And thanks to Bonnie Sicher for listening. To those gifted readers, Tamara Dean, Lexi Freiman, and Cassandra Austin. To my sister Kathy, exchanging tall tales for back rubs, and my brother

Mark, who said to keep looking under the leaf litter. And now thanks to the ones I most wish to please, Holly Willis and you, Eugene Yelchin.

"Freak Weather" first appeared in *Spout;* "So Now Sorrow" in *Pleiades;* "The Way of Affliction" in *EPOCH* magazine; "Deaf Dog" in *Quarter After Eight;* "Animal Control" in *Witness Online;* "In Our House" in *Alaska Quarterly Review;* "Missayings" in *The Greensboro Review,* reprinted in *The Pushcart Prize: Best of the Small Presses;* "To Skin a Rabbit" in *The Brooklyn Review,* reprinted in *Apocalypse 2,* Northeastern Illinois University; "My Husband's Son" in *Alligator Juniper;* "Introduction to Feathers" in *membrane;* "What's to Light" in *Quarter After Eight;* "Not in Nottingham" in *The Normal School.* "Not in Nottingham" was also awarded the *Glimmer Train* Very Short Fiction Prize.